# The Modern
Jewish Experience

# The Modern Jewish Experience

Advisory Editor

**Moses Rischin**

Editorial Board

**Arthur A. Goren**

**Irving Howe**

# THE
# TRAGIC COMEDIANS

BY
GEORGE MEREDITH

**ARNO PRESS**

A New York Times Company

New York / 1975

PR
5006
.M5
1975

Reprint Edition 1975 by Arno Press Inc.

Reprinted from a copy in
 The Newark Public Library

THE MODERN JEWISH EXPERIENCE
ISBN for complete set: 0-405-06690-2
See last pages of this volume for titles.

Manufactured in the United States of America

Library of Congress Cataloging in Publication Data

Meredith, George, 1828-1909.
  The tragic comedians.

  (The Modern Jewish experience)
  Reprint of the 1922 ed. published by Scribner, New
York.
  1. Lassalle, Ferdinand Johann Gottlieb, 1825-1864--
Fiction.  I. Title.  II. Series.
PZ3.M54Tr15  [PR5006]         823'.8         74-29508
ISBN 0-405-06735-6

# TRAGIC COMEDIANS

# THE
# TRAGIC COMEDIANS

### A Study in a Well-Known Story

#### BY
#### GEORGE MEREDITH

**REVISED EDITION**

NEW YORK
CHARLES SCRIBNER'S SONS
1922

COPYRIGHT, 1898, BY
WILLIAM MAXSE MEREDITH

Printed in the United States of America

# THE TRAGIC COMEDIANS

The word "fantastical" is accentuated in our tongue to so scornful an utterance that the constant good service it does would make it seem an appointed instrument for reviewers of books of imaginative matter distasteful to those expository pens. Upon examination, claimants to the epithet will be found outside of books and of poets, in many quarters, Nature being one of the prominent, if not the foremost. Wherever she can get to drink her fill of sunlight she pushes forth fantastically. As for that wandering ship of the drunken pilot, the mutinous crew and the angry captain, called Human Nature, "fantastical" fits it no less completely than a continental baby's skullcap the stormy infant.

Our sympathies, one may fancy, will be broader, our critical acumen shrewder, if we at once accept the thing as a part of us and worthy of study.

The pair of tragic comedians of whom there will be question pass under this word as under their banner and motto. Their acts are incredible: they drank sunlight and drove their bark in a manner to eclipse historical couples upon our planet. Yet they do belong to history, they breathed the stouter air than fiction's, the last chapter of them is written in red blood, and the man pouring out that last chapter was of a mighty nature not unheroical, a man of the active grappling modern brain which wrestles with facts, to keep the world alive, and can create them, to set it spinning.

A Faust-like legend might spring from him: he had a devil. He was the leader of a host, the hope of a party, venerated by his followers, well hated by his enemies, respected by the intellectual chiefs of his time, in the pride of his manhood and his labours when he fell. And why this man should have come to his end through love, and the woman who loved him have laid her hand in the hand of the slayer, is the problem we have to study, nothing inventing, in the spirit and flesh of both. To ask if it was love is useless. Love may be celestial fire before it enters into the systems of mortals. It will then take the character of its place of abode, and we have to look not so much for the pure thing as for the passion. Did it move them, hurry them, animating the giants and gnomes of one, the elves and sprites of the other, and putting animal nature out of its fashionable front rank? The bare railway-line of their story tells of a passion honest enough to entitle it to be related. Nor is there anything invented, because an addition of fictitious incidents could never tell us how she came to do this, he to do that; or how the comic in their natures led by interplay to the tragic issue. They are real creatures, exquisitely fantastical, strangely exposed to the world by a lurid catastrophe, who teach us that fiction, if it can imagine events and persons more agreeable to the taste it has educated, can read us no such furrowing lesson in life.

## CHAPTER I.

An unresisted lady-killer is probably less aware that he roams the pastures in pursuit of a coquette, than is the diligent Arachne that her web is for the devouring lion. At an early age Clotilde von Rüdiger was dissatisfied with her conquests, though they were already numerous in her seventeenth year, for she began precociously, having at her dawn a lively fancy, a womanly person, and singular attractions of colour, eyes, and style. She belonged by birth to the small aristocracy of her native land. Nature had disposed her to coquetry, which is a pastime counting among the arts of fence, and often innocent, often serviceable, though sometimes dangerous, in the centres of polished barbarism known as aristocratic societies, where nature is not absent, but on the contrary very extravagant, tropical, by reason of her idle hours for the imbibing of copious draughts of sunlight. The young lady of charming countenance and sprightly manners is too much besought to choose for her choice to be decided; the numbers beseeching prevent her from choosing instantly, after the fashion of holiday schoolboys crowding a buffet of pastry. These are not coquettish, they clutch what is handy: and little so is the starved damsel of the sequestered village, whose one object of the worldly picturesque is the passing curate; her heart is his for a nod. But to be desired ardently of trooping hosts is an incentive to taste to try for yourself. Men (the jury of householders empanelled to deliver verdicts upon the ways of women) can almost understand that. And as it happens, tasting before you have sounded the sense of your taste will frequently mislead by a step or two difficult to retrieve: the young coquette must then be cruel, as necessarily we kick the waters to escape drowning: and she is not in all cases dealing with simple blocks or limp festoons, she comes upon veteran tricksters that have a knowledge of her sex, capable of outfencing her nascent individuality. The more imagination she has, for a source of strength in the future days, the more is she a prey to the enemy in her time of ignorance.

Clotilde's younger maiden hours and their love episodes are wrapped in the mists Diana considerately drops over her adventurous favourites. She was not under a French mother's rigid supervision. In France the mother resolves that her daughter shall be guarded from the risks of that unequal rencounter between foolish innocence and the predatory. Vigilant foresight is not so much practised where the world is less accurately comprehended. Young people of Clotilde's upper world everywhere, and the young women of it especially, are troubled by an idea drawn from what they inhale and guess at in the spirituous life surrounding them, that the servants of the devil are the valiant host, this world's elect, getting and deserving to get the best it can give in return for a little dashing audacity, a flavour of the Fronde in their conduct; they sin, but they have the world; and then they repent perhaps, but they have had the world. The world is the golden apple. Thirst for it is common during youth: and one would think the French mother worthy of the crown of wisdom if she were not so scrupulously provident in excluding love from the calculations on behalf of her girl.

Say (for Diana's mists are impenetrable and freeze curiosity) that Clotilde was walking with Count Constantine, the brilliant Tartar trained in Paris, when first she met Prince Marko Romaris, at the Hungarian Baths on the borders of the Styrian highlands. The scene at all events is pretty, and weaves a fable out of a variety of floating threads. A stranger to the Baths, dressed in white and scarlet, sprang from his carriage into a group of musical gypsies round an inn at the arch of the chestnut avenue, after pulling up to listen to them for a while. The music had seized him. He snatched bow and fiddle from one of the ring, and with a few strokes kindled their faces. Then seating himself on a bench, he laid the fiddle on his knee, and pinched the strings and flung up his voice, not ceasing to roll out the spontaneous notes when Clotilde and her cavalier, and other couples of the party, came nigh; for he was on the tide of the song, warm in it, and loved it too well to suffer intruders to break the flow, or to think of them. They were close by when the last of it rattled (it was a popular song of a fiery tribe) to its finish. He rose and saluted Clotilde, smiled and jumped back to his carriage, sending a cry of adieu to the swarthy, lank-locked, leather-hued circle, of which his dark oriental eyes and skin of burnished walnut made him look an offshoot, but one of the celestial branch.

He was in her father's reception-room when she reached home: he was paying a visit of ceremony on behalf of his family to General von Rüdiger: which helped her to remember that he had been expected, and also that his favourite colours were known to be white and scarlet. In those very colours, strange to tell, Clotilde was dressed; Prince Marko had recognized her by miraculous divination, he assured her he could have staked his life on the guess as he bowed to her. Adieu to Count Constantine. Fate had interposed the prince opportunely, we have to suppose, for she received a strong impression of his coming straight from her invisible guardian; and the stroke was consequently trenchant which sent the conquering Tartar raving of her fickleness. She struck, like fate, one blow. She discovered that the prince, in addition to his beauty and sweet manners and gift of song, was good; she fell in love with goodness, whereof Count Constantine was not an example: so she set her face another way, soon discovering that there may be fragility in goodness. And now first her imagination conceived the hero who was to subdue her. Could Prince Marko be he, soft as he was, pliable, a docile infant, burning to please her, enraptured in obeying? — the hero who would wrestle with her, overcome and hold her bound? Siegfried could not be dreamed in him, or a Siegfried's baby son-in-arms. She caught a glorious image of the woman rejecting him and his rival, and it informed her that she, dissatisfied with an Adonis, and more than a match for a famous conqueror, was a woman of decisive and independent, perhaps unexampled, force of character. Her idea of a spiritual superiority that could soar over those two men, the bad and the good — the bad because of his vileness, the good because of his frailness — whispered to her of deserving, possibly of attracting, the best of men: the best, that is, in the woman's view of us — the strongest, the great eagle of men, lord of earth and air.

One who will dominate *me*, she thought.

Now when a young lady of lively intelligence and taking charm has brought her mind to believe that she possesses force of character, she persuades the rest of the world easily to agree with her, and so long as her pretensions are not directly opposed to their habits of thought, her parents will be the loudest in proclaiming it, fortifying so the maid's presumption, which is ready to take root in any shadow of subserviency. Her father was a gouty general of infantry in the diplomatic service, disinclined to unnecessary disputes, out of consideration for his vehement irritability when roused. Her mother had been one of the beauties of her set, and was preserving an attenuated reign, through the conversational arts, to save herself from fading into the wall. Her brothers and sisters were not of an age to contest her lead. The temper of the period was revolutionary in society by reflection of the state of politics, and juniors were sturdy democrats, letting their elders know that they had come to their inheritance, while the elders, confused by the impudent topsy-turvy, put on the gaping mask (not unfamiliar to history) of the disestablished conservative, whose astounded state paralyzes his wrath.

Clotilde maintained a decent measure in the liberty she claimed, and it was exercised in wildness of dialogue rather than in capricious behaviour. If her flowing tongue was imperfectly controlled, it was because she discoursed by preference to men upon our various affairs and tangles, and they encouraged her with the tickled wonder which bids the bold advance yet farther into bogland. Becoming the renowned original of her society, wherever it might be, in Germany, Italy, Southern France, she grew chillily sensible of the solitude decreed for their heritage to our loftiest souls. Her Indian Bacchus, as a learned professor supplied Prince Marko's title for her, was a pet, not a companion. She to him was what she sought for in another. As much as she pitied herself for not lighting on the predestined man, she pitied him for having met the woman, so that her tenderness for both inspired many signs of warm affection, not very unlike the thing it moaned secretly the not being. For she could not but distinguish a more poignant sorrow in the seeing of the object we yearn to vainly than in vainly yearning to one unseen. Dressed, to delight him, in Prince Marko's colors, the care she bestowed on her dressing was for the one absent, the shrouded comer: so she pleased the prince to be pleasing to her soul's lord, and this, owing to an appearance of satisfactory deception that it bore, led to her thinking guiltily. We may ask it: an eagle is expected, and how is he to declare his eagleship save by breaking through our mean conventional systems, tearing links asunder, taking his own in the teeth of vulgar ordinances? Clotilde's imagination drew on her reading for the knots it tied and untied, and its ideas of grandeur. Her reading was an interfusion of philosophy skimmed, and realistic romances deep-sounded. She tried hard, but could get no other terrible tangle for her hero's exhibition of flaming azure divineness than the vile one of the wedded woman. Further thinking of it, she revived and recovered; she despised the complication, yet without perceiving how else he was to manifest himself legitimately in a dull modern world. The rescuing her from death would be a poor imitation of worn-out heroes. His publication of a trumpeting book fell appallingly flat in her survey. Deeds of gallantry done as an officer in war (defending his country too) distinguished the soldier, but failed to add the eagle feather to the man. She had a mind of considerable soaring scope, and eclectic: it analyzed a Napoleon, and declined the position of *his* empress. The man must be a gentleman. Poets, princes, warriors, potentates, marched before her speculative fancy unselected.

So far, as far as she can be portrayed introductorily, she is not without exemplars in the sex. Young women have been known to turn from us altogether, never to turn back, so poor and shrunken, or so fleshly-bulgy have we all appeared in the fairy jacket they wove for the right one of us to wear becomingly. But the busy great world was round Clotilde while she was malleable, though she might be losing her fresh ideas of the hammer and the block, and that is a world of much solicitation to induce a vivid girl to merge an ideal in a living image. Supposing, when she has accomplished it, that men justify her choice, the living will retain the colours of the ideal. We have it on record that he may seem an eagle.

"You talk curiously like Alvan, do you know," a gentleman of her country said to her as they were descending the rock of Capri, one day. He said it musingly.

He belonged to a circle beneath her own: the learned and artistic. She had not heard of this Alvan, or had forgotten him; but professing universal knowledge, especially of celebrities, besides having an envious eye for that particular circle, which can pretend to be the choicest of all, she was unwilling to betray her ignorance, and she dimpled her cheek, as one who had often heard the thing said to her before. She smiled musingly.

## CHAPTER II.

"Who is the man they call Alvan?" She put the question at the first opportunity to an aunt of hers.

Up went five-fingered hands. This violent natural sign of horror was comforting: she saw that he was a celebrity indeed.

"Alvan! My dear Clotilde! What on earth can you want to know about a creature who is the worst of demagogues, a disreputable person, and a Jew!"

Clotilde remarked that she had asked only who he was. "Is he clever?"

"He is one of the basest of those wretches who are for upsetting the Throne and Society to gratify their own wicked passions: that is what he is."

"But is he clever?"

"Able as Satan himself, they say. He is a really dangerous, bad man. You could not have been curious about a worse one."

"Politically, you mean."

"Of course I do."

The lady had not thought of any other kind of danger from a man of that station.

The likening of one to Satan does not always exclude meditation upon him. Clotilde was anxious to learn in what way her talk resembled Alvan's. He being that furious creature, she thought of herself at her wildest, which was in her estimation her best; and consequently, she being by no means a furious creature, though very original, she could not meditate on him without softening the outlines given him by report; all because of the likeness between them; and, therefore, as she had knowingly been taken for furious by very foolish people, she settled it that Alvan was also a victim of the prejudices he scorned. It had pleased her at times to scorn our prejudices and feel the tremendous weight she brought on herself by the indulgence. She drew on her recollections of the Satanic in her bosom when so situated, and never having admired herself more ardently than when wearing that aspect, she would have admired the man who had won the frightful title in public, except for one thing — he was a Jew.

The Jew was to Clotilde as flesh of swine to the Jew. Her parents had the same abhorrence of Jewry. One of the favourite similes of the family for whatsoever grunted in grossness, wriggled with meanness, was Jew: and it was noteworthy from the fact that a streak of the blood was in the veins of the latest generation and might have been traced on the maternal side.

Now a meanness that clothes itself in the Satanic to terrify cowards is the vilest form of impudence venturing at insolence; and an insolent impudence with Jew features, the Jew nose and lips, is past endurance repulsive. She dismissed her contemplation of Alvan. Luckily for the gentleman who had compared her to the Jew politician, she did not meet him again in Italy.

She had meanwhile formed an idea of the Alvanesque in dialogue; she summoned her forces to take aim at it, without becoming anything Jewish, still remaining clean and Christian; and by her astonishing practice of the art she could at any time blow up a company — scatter mature and seasoned dames, as had they been balloons on a wind, ay, and give our stout sex a shaking.

Clotilde rejected another aspirant proposed by her parents, and falling into disgrace at home, she went to live for some months with an ancient lady who was her close relative residing in the capital city where the brain of her race is located. There it occurred that a dashing officer of social besides military rank, dancing with her at a ball, said, for a comment on certain boldly independent remarks she had been making: "I see you know Alvan."

Alvan once more.

"Indeed I do not," she said, for she was addressing an officer high above Alvan in social rank; and she shrugged, implying that she was almost past contradiction of the charge.

"Surely you must," said he; "where is the lady who could talk and think as you do without knowing Alvan and sharing his views!"

Clotilde was both startled and nettled.

"But I do not know him at all; I have never met him, never seen him. I am unlikely to meet the kind of person," she protested; and she was amazed yet secretly rejoiced on hearing him, a noble of her own circle, and a dashing officer, rejoin: "Come, come, let us be honest. That is all very well for the little midges floating round us to say of Alvan, but we two can clasp hands and avow proudly that we both know and love the man."

"Were it true, I would own it at once, but I repeat that he is a total stranger to me," she said, seeing the Jew under quite a different illumination.

"Actually?"

"In honour."

"You have never met, never seen him, never read any of his writings?"

"Never. I have heard his name, that is all."

"Then," the officer's voice was earnest, "I pity him, and you no less, while you remain strangers, for you were made for one another. Those ideas you have expressed, nay, the very words, are Alvan's: I have heard him use them. He has just the same original views of society and history as yours; they're identical; your features are not unlike . . . you talk alike: I could fancy your voice the sister of his. You look incredulous? You were speaking of Pompeius, and you said 'Plutarch's Pompeius,' and more — for it is almost incredible under the supposition that you do not know and have never listened to Alvan — you said that Pompeius appeared to have been decorated with all the gifts of the Gods to make the greater sacrifice of him to Cæsar, who was not personally worth a pretty woman's 'bite.' Come, now — you must believe me: at a supper at Alvan's table the other night, the talk happened to be of a modern Cæsar, which led to the real one, and from him to 'Plutarch's Pompeius,' as Alvan called him; and then he said of him what you have just said, absolutely the same down to the allusion to the bite. I assure you. And you have numbers of little phrases in common: you are partners in aphorisms: *Barriers are for those who cannot fly:* that is Alvan's. I could multiply them if I could remember; they struck me as you spoke."

"I must be a shameless plagiarist," said Clotilde.

"Or he," said Count Kollin.

It is here the place of the Chorus to state that these ideas were in the air at the time; sparks of the Vulcanic smithy at work in politics and pervading literature: which both Alvan and Clotilde might catch and give out as their own, in the honest belief that the epigram was original to them. They were not members of a country where literature is confined to its little paddock, without influence on the larger field (part lawn, part marsh) of the social world: they were readers in sympathetic action with thinkers and literary artists. Their saying in common, "Plutarch's Pompeius," may be traceable to a common reading of some professorial article on the portrait-painting of the sage of Chæroneia. The dainty savageness in the "bite" Plutarch mentions, evidently struck on a similarity of tastes in both, as it has done with others. And in regard to Cæsar, Clotilde thought much of Cæsar; she had often wished that Cæsar (for the additional pleasure in thinking of him) had been endowed with the beauty of his rival: one or two of Plutarch's touches upon the earlier history of Pompeius had netted her fancy, faintly (your generosity must be equal to hearing it) stung her blood; she liked the man; and if he had not been beaten in the end, she would have preferred him femininely. His name was not written Pompey to her, as in English, to sound absurd: it was a note of grandeur befitting great and lamentable fortunes, which the young lady declined to share solely because of her attraction to the victor, her compulsion to render unto the victor the sunflower's homage. She rendered it as a slave: the splendid man beloved to ecstasy by the flower of Roman women was her natural choice.

Alvan could not be even a Cæsar in person; he was a Jew. Still a Jew of whom Count Kollin spoke so warmly must be exceptional, and of the exceptional she dreamed. He might have the head of a Cæsar. She imagined a huge head, the cauldron of a boiling brain, anything but bright to the eye, like a pot always on the fire, black, greasy, encrusted, unkempt: the head of a malicious tremendous dwarf. Her hungry inquiries in a city where Alvan was well known, brought her full information of one who enjoyed a highly convivial reputation besides the influence of his political leadership; but no description of his aspect accompanied it, for where he was nightly to be met somewhere about the city, none thought of describing him, and she did not push that question because she had sketched him for herself, and rather wished, the more she heard of his genius, to keep him repulsive. It appeared that his bravery was as well proved as his genius, and a brilliant instance of it had been given in the city not long since. He had her ideas, and he won multitudes with them; he was a talker, a writer, and an orator; and he was learned, while she could not pretend either to learning or to a flow of rhetoric. She could prattle deliciously, at times pointedly, relying on her intuition to tell her more than we get from books, and on her sweet impudence for a richer original strain. She began to appreciate now a reputation for profound acquirements. Learned professors of jurisprudence and history were as enthusiastic for Alvan in their way as Count Kollin. She heard things related of Alvan by the underbreath. That circle below her own, the literary and artistic, idolized him; his talk, his classic breakfasts and suppers, his undisguised ambition, his indomitable energy, his dauntlessness and sway over her sex, were subjects of eulogy all round her; and she heard of an enamoured baroness. No one blamed Alvan. He had shown his chivalrous valour in defending her. The baroness was not a young woman, and she was a hard-bound Blue. She had been the first to discover the prodigy, and had pruned, corrected, and published him; he was one of her political works, promising to be the most successful. An old affair apparently; but the association of a woman's name with Alvan's, albeit the name of a veteran, roused the girl's curiosity, leading her to think his mental and magnetic powers must be of the very highest, considering his physical repulsiveness, for a woman of rank to yield him such extreme devotion. She commissioned her princely serving-man, who had followed and was never far away from her, to obtain precise intelligence of this notorious Alvan.

Prince Marko did what he could to please her; he knew something of the rumours about Alvan and the baroness.

But why should his lady trouble herself for particulars of such people, whom it could scarcely be supposed she would meet by accident? He asked her this. Clotilde said it was common curiosity. She read him a short lecture on the dismal narrowness of their upper world; and on the advantage of taking an interest in the world below them and more enlightened; a world where ideas were current and speech was wine. The prince nodded; if she had these opinions, it must be good for him to have them too, and he shared them, as it were, by the touch of her hand, and for the length of time that he touched her hand, as an electrical shock may be taken by one far removed from the battery, susceptible to it only through the link; he was capable of thinking all that came to him from her a blessing — shocks, wounds and disruptions. He did not add largely to her stock of items, nor did he fetch new colours. The telegraph wire was his model of style. He was more or less a serviceless Indian Bacchus, standing for sign of the beauty and vacuity of their world: and how dismally narrow that world was, she felt with renewed astonishment at every dive out of her gold-fish pool into the world of tides below; so that she was ready to scorn the cultivation of the graces, and had, when not submitting to the smell, fanciful fits of a liking for tobacco smoke — the familiar incense of those homes where speech was wine.

At last she fell to the asking of herself whether, in the same city with him, often among his friends, hearing his latest intimate remarks — things homely redolent of him as hot bread of the oven — she was ever to meet this man upon whom her thoughts were bent to the eclipse of all others. She desired to meet him for comparison's sake, and to criticise a popular hero. It was inconceivable that any one popular could approach her standard, but she was curious; flame played about him; she had some expectation of easing a spiteful sentiment created by the recent subjection of her thoughts to the prodigious little Jew; and some feeling of closer pity for Prince Marko she had, which urged her to be rid of her delusion as to the existence of a wonder-working man on our earth, that she might be sympathetically kind to the prince, perhaps com-

pliant, and so please her parents, be good and dull, and
please everybody, and adieu to dreams, good night, and
so to sleep with the beasts! . . .

Calling one afternoon on a new acquaintance of the
flat table-land she liked tripping down to from her heights,
Clotilde found the lady in supreme toilette, glowing,
bubbling: "Such a breakfast, my dear!" The costly pro-
fusion, the anecdotes, the wit, the fun, the copious
draughts of the choicest of life — was there ever anything
to match it? Never in that lady's recollection, or her
husband's either, she exclaimed. And where was the
breakfast? Why, at Alvan's, to be sure; where else could
such a breakfast be?

"And you know Alvan!" cried Clotilde, catching excitement from the lady's flush.

"Alvan is one of my husband's closest friends."

Clotilde put on the playful frenzy; she made show of
wringing her hands: "Oh! happy you! you know Alvan?
And everybody is to know him except me? why? I proclaim it unjust. Because I am unmarried? I'll take a
husband to-morrow morning to be entitled to meet Alvan
in the evening."

The playful frenzy is accepted in its exact innocent
signification of "this is my pretty wilful will and way,"
and the lady responded to it cordially; for it is pleasant
to have some one to show, and pleasant to assist some one
eager to see: besides, many had petitioned her for a sight
of Alvan; she was used to the request.

"You're not obliged to wait for to-morrow," she said.
"Come to one of our gatherings to-night. Alvan will be
here."

"You invite me?"

"Distinctly. Pray, come. He is sure to be here.
We have his promise, and Alvan never fails. Was it not
Frau v. Crestow who did us the favour of our introduction?
She will bring you."

The Frau v. Crestow was a cousin of Clotilde's by marriage, sentimental, but strict in her reading of the pro-
prieties. She saw nothing wrong in undertaking to
conduct Clotilde to one of those famous gatherings of the
finer souls of the city and the race; and her husband

agreed to join them after the sitting of the Chamber upon a military-budget vote. The whole plan was nicely arranged and went well. Clotilde dressed carefully, letting her gold-locks cloud her fine forehead carelessly, with finishing touches to the negligence, for she might be challenged to take part in disputations on serious themes, and a handsome young woman who has to sustain an argument against a man does wisely when she forearms her beauties for a reserve, to carry out flanking movements if required. The object is to beat him.

## CHAPTER III.

HER hostess met her at the entrance of the rooms, murmuring that Alvan was present, and was *there:* — a direction of a nod that any quick-witted damsel must pretend to think sufficient, so Clotilde slipped from her companion and gazed into the recess of a doorless inner room, where three gentlemen stood, backed by book-cases, conversing in blue vapours of tobacco. They were indistinct; she could see that one of them was of good stature. One she knew; he was the master of the house, mildly Jewish. The third was distressingly branded with the slum and gutter signs of the Ahasuerus race. Three hats on his head could not have done it more effectively. The vindictive caricatures of the God Pan, executed by priests of the later religion burning to hunt him out of worship in the semblance of the hairy, hoofy, snouty Evil One, were not more loathsome. She sank on a sofa. That the man? Oh! Jew, and fifty times over Jew! nothing but Jew!

The three stepped into the long saloon, and she saw how veritably magnificent was the first whom she had noticed.

She sat at her lamb's-wool work in the little ivory frame, feeding on the contrast. This man's face was the born orator's, with the light-giving eyes, the forward nose, the animated mouth, all stamped for speechfulness and enterprise, of Cicero's rival in the forum before he took the headship of armies and marched to empire. The gifts of speech, enterprise, decision, were marked on his features and his bearing, but with a fine air of lordly mildness. Alas, he could not be other than Christian, so glorious was he in build! One could vision an eagle swooping to his helm by divine election. So vigorously rich was his blood that the swift emotion running with the theme as he talked pictured itself in passing and was like the play of sheet lightning on the variations of the uninterrupted and many-glancing outpour. Looking on him was listening. Yes, the looking on him sufficed. Here was an image of the beauty of a new order of godlike men, that drained an Indian Bacchus of his thin seductions at a breath — reduced him to the state of nursery plaything, spangles and wax, in the contemplation of a girl suddenly plunged on the deeps of her womanhood. She shrank to smaller and smaller as she looked.

Be sure that she knew who he was. No, says she. But she knew. It terrified her soul to think he was Alvan. She feared scarcely less that it might not be he. Between these dreads of doubt and belief she played at cat and mouse with herself, escaped from cat, persecuted mouse, teased herself, and gloated. It is he! not he! he! not he! most certainly! impossible! — And then it ran: If he, oh me! If another, woe me! For she had come to see Alvan. Alvan and she shared ideas. They talked marvellously alike, so as to startle Count Kollin: and supposing he was not Alvan, it would be a bitter disappointment. The supposition that he was, threatened her with instant and life-long bondage.

Then again, could that face be the face of a Jew? She feasted. It was a noble profile, an ivory skin, most lustrous eyes. Perchance a Jew of the Spanish branch of the exodus, not the Polish. There is the noble Jew as well as the bestial Gentile. There is not in the sublimest of Gentiles a majesty comparable to that of the Jew elect. He may well think his race favoured of heaven, though heaven chastise them still. The noble Jew is grave in age, but in his youth he is the arrow to the bow of his fiery eastern blood, and in his manhood he is — ay, what you see there! a figure of easy and superb preponderance, whose fire has mounted to inspirit and be tempered by the intellect.

She was therefore prepared all the while for the surprise of learning that the gentleman so unlike a Jew was Alvan; and she was prepared to express her recordation of the circumstance in her diary with phrases of very eminent surprise. Necessarily it would be the greatest of surprises.

The three, this man and his two of the tribe, upon whom Clotilde's attention centred, with a comparison in her mind too sacred to be other than profane (comparisons will thrust themselves on minds disordered), dropped to the cushions of the double-seated sofa, by one side of which she cowered over her wool-work, willing to dwindle to a pin's head if her insignificance might enable her to hear the words of the speaker. He pursued his talk: there was little danger of not hearing him. There was only the danger of feeling too deeply the spell of his voice. His voice had the mellow fulness of the clarionet. But for the subject, she could have fancied a noontide piping of great Pan by the sedges. She had never heard a continuous monologue so musical, so varied in music, amply-flowing, vivacious, interwovenly the brook, the stream, the torrent: a perfect natural orchestra in a single instrument. He had notes less pastorally imageable, notes that fired the blood, with the ranging of his theme. The subject became clearer to her subjugated wits, until the mental vivacity he roused on certain impetuous phrases of assertion caused her pride to waken up and rebel as she took a glance at herself, remembering that she likewise was a thinker, deemed in her society an original thinker, an intrepid thinker and talker, not so very much beneath this man in audacity of brain, it might be. He kindled her thus, and the close-shut bud expanded and knew the fretting desire to breathe out the secret within it, and be appreciated in turn.

The young flower of her sex burned to speak, to deliver an opinion. She was unaccustomed to yield a fascinated ear. She was accustomed rather to dictate and be the victorious performer, and though now she was not anxious to occupy the pulpit – being too strictly bred to wish for a post publicly in any of the rostra — and meant still less to dispossess the present speaker of the place he filled so well, she yearned to join him: and as that could not be done by a stranger approving, she panted to dissent. A young lady cannot so well say to an unknown gentleman: "You have spoken truly, sir," as, "That is false!" for to speak in the former case would be gratuitous, and in the latter she is excused by the moral warmth provoking her. Further, dissent rings out finely, and approval is a feeble murmur — a poor introduction of oneself. Her moral warmth was ready and waiting for the instigating subject, but of course she was unconscious of the goad within. Excitement wafted her out of herself, as we say, or out of the conventional vessel into the waves of her troubled nature. He had not yet given her an opportunity for dissenting; she was compelled to agree, dragged at his chariot-wheels in headlong agreement.

His theme was Action; the political advantages of Action; and he illustrated his view with historical examples, to the credit of the French, the temporary discredit of the German and English races, who tend to compromise instead. Of the English he spoke as of a power extinct, a people "gone to fat," who have gained their end in a hoard of gold and shut the door upon bandit ideas. Action means life to the soul as to the body. Compromise is virtual death: it is the pact between cowardice and comfort under the title of expediency. So do we gather dead matter about us. So are we gradually self-stifled, corrupt. The war with evil in every form must be incessant: we cannot have peace. Let then our joy be in war; in uncompromising Action, which need not be the less a sagacious conduct of the war. . . . Action energizes men's brains, generates grander capacities, provokes greatness of soul between enemies, and is the guarantee of positive conquest for the benefit of our species. To doubt that, is to doubt of good being to be had for the seeking. He drew pictures of the healthy Rome when turbulent, the doomed quiescent. Rome struggling grasped the world. Rome stagnant invited Goth and Vandal. So forth: alliterative antitheses of the accustomed pamphleteer. At last her chance arrived.

His opposition sketch of Inaction was refreshed by an

analysis of the character of Hamlet. Then he reverted to Hamlet's promising youth. How brilliantly endowed was the Prince of Denmark in the beginning!

"Mad from the first!" cried Clotilde.

She produced an effect not unlike that of a sudden crack of thunder. The three made chorus in a noise of boots on the floor.

Her hero faced about and stood up, looking at her fulgently. Their eyes engaged without wavering on either side. Brave eyes they seemed, each pair of them, for his were fastened on a comely girl, and she had strung herself to her gallantest to meet the crisis.

His friends quitted him at a motion of the elbows. He knelt on the sofa, leaning across it, with clasped hands.

"You are she! — So, then, is a contradiction of me to be the commencement?"

"After the apparition of Hamlet's father the prince was mad," said Clotilde, hurriedly, and she gazed for her hostess, a paroxysm of alarm succeeding that of her boldness.

"Why should we two wait to be introduced?" said he. "We know one another. I am Alvan. You are she of whom I heard from Kollin: who else? Lucretia the gold-haired; the gold-crested serpent, wise as her sire; Aurora breaking the clouds; in short, Clotilde!"

Her heart exulted to hear him speak her name. She laughed with a radiant face. His being Alvan, and his knowing her and speaking her name, all was like the happy reading of a riddle. He came round to her, bowing, and his hand out. She gave hers: she could have said, if asked, "For good!" And it looked as though she had given it for good.

## CHAPTER IV.

"HAMLET in due season," said he, as they sat together. "I shall convince you."

She shook her head.

"Yes, yes, an opinion formed by a woman is inflexible; I know that: the fact is not half so stubborn. But at present there are two more important actors: we are not at Elsinore. You are aware that I hoped to meet you?"

"Is there a periodical advertisement of your hopes? — or do they come to us by intuition?"

"Kollin was right! — the ways of the serpent will be serpentine. I knew we must meet. It is no true day so long as the goddess of the morning and the sungod are kept asunder. I speak of myself, by what I have felt since I heard of you."

"You are sure of your divinity?"

"Through my belief in yours!"

They bowed smiling at the courtly exchanges.

"And tell me," said he, "as to meeting me? . . ."

She replied: "When we are so like the rest of the world we may confess our weakness."

"Unlike! for the world and I meet and part: not we two."

Clotilde attempted an answer: it would not come. She tried to be revolted by his lording tone, and found it strangely inoffensive. His lording presence and the smile that was like a waving feather on it compelled her so strongly to submit to hear, as to put her in danger of appearing to embrace this man's rapid advances.

She said: "I first heard of you at Capri."

"And I was at Capri seven days after you had left."

"You knew my name *then*?"

"Be not too curious with necromancers. Here is the date — March 15th. You departed on the 8th."

"I think I did. That is a year from now."

"Then we missed: now we meet. It is a year lost. A year is a great age! Reflect on it and what you owe me. How I wished for a comrade at Capri! Not a 'young lady,' and certainly no man. The understanding Feminine was my desire — a different thing from the feminine understanding, usually. I wanted my comrade young and fair, necessarily of your sex, but with heart and brain: an insane request, I fancied, until I heard that you were the person I wanted. In default of you I paraded the island with Tiberius, who is my favourite tyrant. We took the initiative against the patricians, at my suggestion, and the Annals were written by a plebeian demagogue, instead of by one of that party, whose account of my extinction by command of the emperor was pathetic. He apologized in turn for my imperial master and me, saying truly, that the misunderstanding between us was past cement: for each of us loved the man but hated his office; and as the man is always more in his office than he is in himself, clearly it was the lesser portion of our friend that each of us loved. So, I, as the weaker, had to perish, as he would have done had I been the stronger; I admitted it, and sent my emperor my respectful adieux, with directions for the avoiding of assassins. Mademoiselle, by delaying your departure seven days, you would have saved me from death. You see, the official is the artificial man, and I ought to have known there is no natural man left in us to weigh against the artificial. I counted on the emperor's personal affection, forgetting that princes cannot be our friends."

"You died bravely?"

Clotilde entered into the extravagance with a happy simulation of zest.

"Simply, we will say. My time had come, and I took no sturdy pose, but let the life-stream run its course for a less confined embankment. Sapphire sea, sapphire sky: one believes in life there, thrills with it, when life is ebbing: ay, as warmly as when life is at the flow in our sick and shrivelled North — the climate for dried fish! Verily the second death of hearing that a gold-haired Lucretia had been on the island seven days earlier, was harder to bear. Tell me frankly — the music in Italy?"

"Amorous and martial, brainless and monotonous."

"Excellent!" his eyes flashed delightedly. "O comrade of comrades! that year lost to me will count heavily as I learn to value those I have gained. Yes, brainless! There, in music, we beat them, as politically France beats us. No life without brain! The brainless in Art and in Statecraft are nothing but a little more obstructive than the dead. It is less easy to cut a way through them. But it must be done, or the Philistine will be as the locust in his increase, and devour the green blades of the earth. You have been trained to shudder at the démagogue?"

"I do not shudder," said Clotilde.

"A diamond from the lapidary! — Your sentences have many facets. Well, you are conversing with a demagogue, an avowed one: a demagogue and a Jew. You take it as a matter of course: you should exhibit some sparkling incredulity. The Christian is like the politician in supposing the original obverse of him everlastingly the same, after the pattern of the monster he was originally taught to hate. But the Jew has been a little christianized, and we have a little bejewed the Christian. So with demagogues: as we see the conservative crumbling, we grow conservatived. Try to think individually upon what you have to learn collectively — that is your task. You are of the few who will be equal to it. We are not men of blood, believe me. I am not. For example, I detest and I decline the duel. I have done it, and proved myself a man of metal notwithstanding. To say nothing of the inhumanity, the senselessness of duelling revolts me. 'T is a folly, so your nobles practise it, and your royal wiseacre sanctions. No blood for me: and yet I tell you that whatever opposes me, I will sweep away. How? With the brain. If we descend to poor brute strength or brutal craft, it is from failing in the brain: we quit the leadership of our forces, and the descent is the beast's confession. Do I say how? Perhaps by your aid. — You do not start and cry: 'Mine!' That is well. I have not much esteem for non-professional actresses. They are numerous and not entertaining. — You leave it to me to talk."

"Could I do better?"

"You listen sweetly."

"It is because I like to hear."

"You have the pearly little ear of a shell on the sand."

"With the great sea sounding near it!"

Alvan drew closer to her.

"I look into your eyes and perceive that one may listen to you and speak to you. Heart to heart, then! Yes, a sea to lull you, a sea to win you — temperately, let us hope; by storm, if need be. My prize is found! The good friend who did the part of Iris for us came bounding to me: 'I have discovered the wife for you, Alvan.' I had previously heard of her from another as having touched the islet of Capri. 'But,' said Kollin, 'she is a gold-crested serpent — slippery!' Is she? That only tells me of a little more to be mastered. I feel my future now. Hitherto it has been a land without sunlight. Do you know how the look of sunlight on a land calms one? It signifies to the eye possession and repose, the end gained — not the end to labour, just heaven! but peace to the heart's craving, which is the renewal of strength for work, the fresh dip in the waters of life. Conjure up your vision of Italy. Remember the meaning of Italian light and colour: the clearness, the luminous fulness, the thoughtful shadows. Mountain and wooded headland are solid, deep to the eye, spirit-speaking to the mind. They throb. You carve shapes of gods out of that sky, the sea, those peaks. They live with you. How they satiate the vacant soul by influx, and draw forth the troubled from its prickly nest! — Well, and you are my sunlighted land. And you will have to be fought for. And I see not the less repose in the prospect! Part of you may be shifty — sand. The sands are famous for their golden shining — as you shine. Well, then, we must make the quicksands concrete. I have a perfect faith in you, and in the winning of you. Clearly you will have to be fought for. I should imagine it a tough battle to come. But as I doubt neither you nor myself, I see beyond it. — We use phrases in common, and aphorisms, it appears. Why? but that our minds act in unison. What if I were to make a comparison of you with Paris? — the city of Paris, Lutetia."

"Could you make it good?" said Clotilde.

He laughed and postponed it for a series of skimming discussions, like swallow-flights from the nest beneath the eaves to the surface of the stream, perpetually reverting to her, and provoking spirited replies, leading her to fly with him in expectation of a crowning compliment that must be singular and was evidently gathering confirmation in his mind from the touchings and probings of her character on these flights.

She was like a lady danced off her sense of fixity, to whom the appearance of her whirling figure in the mirror is both wonderful and reassuring; and she liked to be discussed, to be compared to anything, for the sake of being the subject, so as to be sure it was she that listened to a man who was a stranger, claiming her for his own; sure it was she that by not breaking from him implied consent, she that went speeding in this magical rapid round which slung her more and more out of her actual into her imagined self, compelled her to proceed, denied her the right to faint and call upon the world for aid, and catch at it, though it was close by and at a signal would stop the terrible circling. The world was close by and had begun to stare. She half apprehended that fact, but she was in the presence of the irresistible. In the presence of the irresistible the conventional is a crazy structure swept away with very little creaking of its timbers on the flood. When we feel its power we are immediately primitive creatures, flying anywhere in space, indifferent to nakedness. And after trimming ourselves for it, the sage asks your permission to add, it will be the thing we are most certain some day to feel. Had not she trimmed herself? — so much that she had won fame for an originality mistaken by her for the independent mind, and perilously, for courage. She had trimmed herself and Alvan too — herself to meet it, and Alvan to be it. Her famous originality was a trumpet blown abroad proclaiming her the prize of the man who sounded as loudly his esteem for the quality — in a fair young woman of good breeding. Each had evoked the other. Their common anticipations differed in this, that he had expected comeliness, she the reverse — an Esau of the cities; and seeing superb manly beauty in the place of the thick-featured sodden satyr of her miscreating fancy, the irresistible was revealed to her on its divinest whirlwind.

They both desired beauty; they had each stipulated for beauty before captivity could be acknowledged; and he beholding her very attractive comeliness, walked into the net, deeming the same a light thing to wear, and rather a finishing grace to his armory; but she, a trained disciple of the conventional in social behaviour (as to the serious points and the extremer trifles), fluttered exceedingly; she knew not what she was doing, where her hand was, how she looked at him, how she drank in his looks on her. Her woman's eyes had no guard: they had scarcely speculation. She saw nothing in its passing, but everything backward, under haphazard flashes. The sight of her hand disengaged told her it had been detained; a glance at the company reminded her that those were men and women who had been other than phantoms; recollections of the words she listened to, assented to, replied to, displayed the gulfs she had crossed. And nevertheless her brain was as quick as his to press forward to pluck the themes which would demonstrate her mental vividness and at least indicate her force of character. The splendour of the man quite extinguished, or over-brightened, her sense of personal charm; she set fire to her brain to shine intellectually, treating the tale of her fair face as a childish tale that might have a grain of truth in it, some truth, a very little, and that little nearly worthless, merely womanly, a poor charm of her sex. The intellectual endowment was rarer: still rarer the moral audacity. O, to match this man's embracing discursiveness! his ardour, his complacent energy, the full strong sound he brought out of all subjects! He struck, and they rang. There was a bell in everything for him; Nature gave out her cry, and significance was on all sides of the universe; no dead stuff, no longer any afflicting lumpishness. His brain was vivifying light. And how humane he was! how supremely tolerant! Where she had really thought instead of flippantly tapping at the doors of thought, or crying vagrantly for an echo, his firm footing in the region thrilled her; and where she had felt deeper than fancifully, his wise tenderness overwhelmed. Strange to consider: with all his precious gifts, which must make the gift of life thrice dear to him, he was fearless. Less by what he said than by divination she discerned that he knew not fear. If for only that, she would have hung to him like his shadow. She could have detected a brazen pretender. A meaner mortal vaunting his great stores she would have written down coxcomb. Her social training and natural perception raised her to a height to measure the bombastical and distinguish it from the eloquently lofty. He spoke of himself, as the towering Alp speaks out at a first view, bidding that which he was be known. Fearless, confident, able, he could not but be, as he believed himself, indomitable. She who was this man's mate would consequently wed his possessions, including courage. Clotilde at once reached the conclusion of her having it in an equal degree. Was she not displaying it? The worthy people of the company stared, as she now perceived, and she was indifferent; her relatives were present without disturbing her exaltation. She wheeled above their heads in the fiery chariot beside her sungod. It could not but be courage, active courage, superior to her previous tentative steps — the verbal temerities she had supposed so dauntless. For now she was in action, now she was being tried to match the preacher and incarnation of the virtues of action!

Alvan shaped a comparison of her with Paris, his beloved of cities — the symbolized goddess of the lightning brain that is quick to conceive, eager to realize ideas, impassioned for her hero, but ever putting him to proof, graceful beyond all rhyme, colloquial as never the Muse; light in light hands, yet valiant unto death for a principle; and therefore not light, anything but light in strong hands, very steadfast rather: and oh! constantly entertaining.

The comparison had to be strained to fit the living lady's shape. Did he think it, or a dash of something like it?

His mood was luxurious. He had found the fair and youthful original woman of refinement and station desired by him. He had good reason to wish to find her. Having won a name, standing on firm ground, with promise of a great career, chief of what was then taken for a growing party and is not yet a collapsed, nor will be, though the foot on it is iron, his youth had flown under the tutelage of an extraordinary Mentor, whom to call Athene robs the goddess of her personal repute for wisdom in conduct, but whose head was wise, wise as it was now grey. Verily she was original; and a grey original should seem remarkable above a blooming blonde. If originality in woman were our prime request, the grey should bear the palm. She has gone through the battle, retaining the standard she carried into it, which is a victory. Alas, that grey, so spirit-touching in Art, should be so wintry in reality!

The discovery of a feminine original breathing Spring,

softer, warmer than the ancient one, gold instead of snow crested, and fully as intrepid as devoted, was an immense joy to Alvan. He took it luxuriously because he believed in his fortune, a kind of natal star, the common heritage of the adventurous, that brought him his good things in time, in return for energetic strivings in a higher direction apart from his natural longings. Fortune had delayed, he had wintered long. All the sweeter was the breath of the young Spring. That exquisite new sweetness robed Clotilde in the attributes of the person dreamed of for his mate; and deductively assuming her to possess them, he could not doubt his power of winning her. *Barriers are for those who cannot fly.* The barriers were palpable about a girl of noble Christian birth: so was the courage in her which would give her wings, he thought, coming to that judgement through the mixture of his knowledge of himself and his perusal of her exterior. He saw that she could take an impression deeply enough to express it sincerely, and he counted on it, sympathetically endowing her with his courage to support the originality she was famed for.

They were interrupted between whiles by weariful men running to Alvan for counsel on various matters — how to play their game, or the exact phrasing of some pregnant sentence current in politics or literature. He satisfied them severally and shouldered them away, begging for peace that night. Clotilde corroborated his accurate recital of the lines of a contested verse of the incomparable Heinrich, and they fell to capping verses of the poet — lucid metheglin, with here and there no dubious flavour of acid, and a lively sting in the tail of the honey. Sentiment, cynicism, and satin impropriety and scabrous, are among those verses, where pure poetry has a recognized voice; but the lower elements constitute the popularity in a cultivated society inclining to wantonness out of bravado as well as by taste. Alvan, looking indolently royal and royally roguish, quoted a verse that speaks of the superfluousness of a faithless lady's vowing bite:

"The kisses were in the course of things,
The *bite* was a needless addition."

Clotilde could not repress her reddening — Count Kollin had repeated too much! She dropped her eyes, with a face of sculpture, then resumed their chatter. He spared her the allusion to Pompeius. She convinced him of her capacity for reserve besides intrepidity, and flattered him too with her blush. She could dare to say to Kollin what her scarlet sensibility forbade her touching on with him: not that she would not have had an airy latitude with him to touch on what she pleased; he liked her for her boldness and the cold peeping of the senses displayed in it: he liked also the distinction she made.

The cry to supper conduced to a further insight of her adaptation to his requirements in a wife. They marched to the table together, and sat together, and drank a noble Rhine wine together — true Rauenthal. His robustness of body and soul inspired the wish that his well-born wife might be, in her dainty fashion, yet honestly and without mincing, his possible boonfellow: he and she, glass in hand, thanking the bountiful heavens, blessing mankind in chorus. It belonged to his hearty dream of the wife he would choose, were she to be had. The position of interpreter of heaven's benevolence to mankind through his own enjoyment of the gifts, was one that he sagaciously demanded for himself, sharing it with the Philistine unknowingly; and to have a wife no less wise than he on this throne of existence was a rosy exaltation. Clotilde kindled to the hint of his festival mood of Solomon at the banquet. She was not devoid of a discernment of flavours; she had heard grave judges at her father's board profoundly deliver their verdicts upon this and that vineyard and vintage; and it is a note of patriotism in her country to be enthusiastic for wine of the Rhine: she was, moreover, thirsty from much talking and excitement. She drank her glass relishingly, declaring the wine princely. Alvan smacked his hands in a rapture: "You are not for the extract of raisin our people have taken to copy from French Sauternes, to suit a female predilection for sugar?"

"No, no, the grape for me!" said she: "the Rhine grape with the elf in it, and the silver harp and the stained legend!"

"Glorious!"

He toasted the grape. "Wine of the grape is the young bride — the young sun-bride! divine, and never too sweet, never cloying like the withered sun-*dried*, with its one drop of concentrated sugar, that becomes ten of gout. No raisin-juice for us! None of their too-long-on-the-stem clusters! We are for the blood of the grape in her youth, her heaven-kissing ardour. I have a cellar charged with the bravest of the Rhine. We — will we not assail it, bleed it in the gallant days to come? we two!" The picture of his bride and him drinking the sun down after a day of savage toil was in the shout — a burst unnoticed in the incessantly verbalizing buzz of a continental supper-table. Clotilde acquiesced: she chimed to it like a fair boonfellow of the rollicking faun. She was realizing fairyland.

They retired to the divan-corner where it was you-and-I between them as with rivulets meeting and branching, running parallel, uniting and branching again, divided by the theme, but unending in the flow of the harmony. So ran their chirping arguments and diversions. The carrying on of a prolonged and determined you-and-I in company intimates to those undetermined floating atoms about us that a certain sacred something is in process of formation, or has formed; and people looked, and looked hard at the pair, and at one another afterward: none approached them. The Signor conjuror who has a thousand arts for conjuring with nature was generally considered to have done that night his most ancient and reputedly fabulous trick — the dream of poets, rarely witnessed anywhere, and almost too wonderful for credence in a haunt of our later civilization. Yet there it was: the sudden revelation of the intense divinity to a couple fused in oneness by his apparition, could be perceived of all having man and woman in them; love at first sight was visible. "Who ever loved that loved not at first sight?" And if nature, character, circumstance, and a maid clever at dressing her mistress's golden hair, did prepare them for Love's lighting-match, not the less were they proclaimingly alight and in full blaze. Likewise, Time, imperious old gentleman though we know him to be, with his fussy reiterations concerning the hour for bed and sleep, bowed to the magical fact of their condition, and forbore to warn them of his passing from night to day. He had to go, he must, he has to be always going, but as long as he could he left them on their bank by the margin of the stream, where a shadow-cycle of the eternal wound a circle for them and allowed them to imagine they had thrust that old driver of the dusty high-road quietly out of the way. They were ungrateful, of course, when the performance of his duties necessitated his pulling them up beside him pretty smartly, but he uttered no prophecy of ever intending to rob them of the celestial moments they had cut from him and meant to keep between them "for ever," and fresh.

The hour was close on the dawn of a March morning. Alvan assisted at the cloaking and hooding of Clotilde. Her relatives were at hand; they hung by while he led her to the stairs and down into a spacious moonlight that laid the traceries of the bare tree-twigs clear-black on grass and stone.

"A night to head the Spring!" said Alvan. "Come."

He lifted her off the steps and set her on the ground, as one who had an established right to the privilege: and she did not contest it, nor did her people, so kingly was he, arrayed in the thunder of the bolt which had struck the pair. These things, and many things that islands know not of, are done upon continents, where perhaps traditions of the awfulness of Love remain more potent in society; or it may be, that an island atmosphere dispossesses the bolt of its promptitude to strike, or the breastplates of the islanders are strengthened to resist the bolt, or no tropical heat is there to create and launch it, or nothing is to be seen of it for the haziness, or else giants do not walk there. But even where he walked, amid a society intellectually fostering sentiment, in a land bowing to see the simplicity of the mystery paraded, Alvan's behaviour was passing heteroclite. He needed to be the kingly fellow he was, crowned by another kingly fellow — the lord of hearts — to impose it uninterruptedly. "She is mine; I have won her this night!" his bearing said; and Clotilde's acquiesced; and the worthy couple following them had to exhibit a copy of the same, much wondering. Partly by habit, and of his natural astuteness, Alvan peremptorily usurped a lead that once taken could not easily be challenged, and would roll him on a good tideway strong in his own passion and his lady's up against the last defences — her parents. A difficulty with them was foreseen. What is a difficulty! — a gate in the hunting-field: an opponent on a platform: a knot beneath a sword: the dam to waters that draw from the heavens. Not desiring it in this case — it would have been to love the difficulty better than the woman — he still enjoyed the bracing prospect of a resistance, if only because it was a portion of the dowry she brought him. Good soldiers (who have won their grades) are often of a peaceful temper and would not raise an invocation to war, but a view of the enemy sets their pugnacious forces in motion, the bugle fills their veins with electrical fire, till they are as racers on the race-course. His inmost hearty devil was glad of a combat that pertained to his possession of her, for battle gives the savour of the passion to win, and victory dignifies a prize: he was, however, resolved to have it, if possible, according to the regular arrangement of such encounters, formal, without snatchings, without rash violence; a victory won by personal ascendancy, reasoning eloquence.

He laughed to hear her say, in answer to a question as to her present feelings: "I feel that I am carried away by a centaur!" The comparison had been used or implied to him before.

"No!" said he, responding to a host of memories, to shake them off, "no more of the quadruped man! You tempt him — may I tell you that? Why, now, this moment, at the snap of my fingers, what is to hinder our taking the short cut to happiness, centaur and nymph? One leap and a gallop, and we should be into the morning, leaving night to grope for us, parents and friends to run about for the wits they lose in running. But no! No more scandals. That silver moon invites us by its very spell of bright serenity, to be mad: just as, when you drink of a reverie, the more prolonged it is the greater the readiness for wild delirium at the end of the draught. But no!" his voice deepened — "the handsome face of the orb that lights us would be well enough were it only a gallop between us two. Dearest, the orb that lights us two for a lifetime must be taken all round, and I have been on the wrong side of the moon: I have seen the other face of it — a visage scored with regrets, dead dreams, burnt passions, bald illusions, and the like, the like! — sunless, waterless, without a flower! It is the old volcano land: it grows one bitter herb: if ever you see my mouth distorted you will know I am revolving a taste of it; and as I need the antidote you give, I will not be the centaur to win you, for that is the land where he stables himself; yes, there he ends his course, and that is the herb he finishes by pasturing on. You have no dislike of metaphors and parables? We Jews are a parable people."

"I am sure I do understand . . ." said Clotilde, catching her breath to be conscientious, lest he should ask her for an elucidation.

"Provided always that the metaphor be not like the metaphysician's treatise on Nature: a torch to see the sunrise! — You were going to add — ?"

"I was going to say, I think I understand, but you run away with me still."

"May the sensation never quit you!"

"It will not."

"What a night!" Alvan raised his head: "A night cast for our first meeting and betrothing! You are near home?"

"The third house yonder in the moonlight."

"The moonlight lays a white hand on it!"

"That is my window sparkling."

"That is the vestal's cresset. Shall I blow it out?"

"You are too far. And it is a celestial flame, sir!"

"Celestial in truth! My hope of heaven! Dian's crescent will be ever on that house for me, Clotilde. I would it were leagues distant, or the door not forbidden!"

"I could minister to a good knight humbly."

Alvan bent to her, on a sudden prompting:

"When do father and mother arrive?"

"To-morrow."

He took her hand. "To-morrow, then! The worst of omens is delay."

Clotilde faintly gasped. Could he mean it? — he of so evil a name in her family and circle!

Her playfulness and pleasure in the game of courtliness forsook her.

"Tell me the hour when it will be most convenient to them to receive me," said Alvan.

She stopped walking in sheer fright.

"My father — my mother?" she said, imaging within her the varied horror of each and the commotion.

"To-morrow or the day after — not later. No delays! You are mine, we are one; and the sooner my cause is pleaded the better for us both. If I could step in and see them this instant, it would be forestalling mischances. Do you not see, that time is due to us, and the minutes are our gold slipping away?"

She shrank her hand back: she did not wish to withdraw the hand, only to shun the pledge it signified. He opened an abyss at her feet, and in deadly alarm of him she exclaimed: "Oh! not yet; not immediately." She trembled, she made her petition dismal by her anguish of speechlessness. "There will be such . . . not yet! Perhaps later. They must not be troubled yet — at present. I am . . . I cannot — pray, delay!"

"But you are mine!" said Alvan. "You feel it as I do. There can be no real impediment?"

She gave an empty sigh that sought to be a run of entreaties. In fear of his tongue she caught at words to baffle it, senseless of their imbecility: "Do not insist: yes, in time: they will — they — they may. My father is not very well . . . my mother: she is not very well. They are neither of them very well: not at present! — Spare them at present."

To avoid being carried away, she flung herself from the centaur's back to the disenchanting earth; she separated herself from him in spirit, and beheld him as her father and mother and her circle would look on this pretender to her hand, with his lordly air, his Jew blood, and his hissing reputation — for it was a reputation that stirred the snakes and the geese of the world. She saw him in their eyes, quite coldly: which imaginative capacity was one of the remarkable feats of cowardice, active and cold of brain even while the heart is active and would be warm.

He read something of her weakness. "And supposing I decide that it must be?"

"How can I supplicate you!" she replied with a shiver, feeling that she had lost her chance of slipping from his grasp, as trained women of the world, or very sprightly young wits know how to do at the critical moment: and she had lost it by being too sincere. Her cowardice appeared to her under that aspect.

"Now I perceive that the task is harder," said Alvan, seeing her huddled in a real dismay. "Why will you not rise to my level and fear nothing! The way is clear: we have only to take the step. Have you not seen to-night that we are fated for one another? It is your destiny, and trifling with destiny is a dark business. Look at me. Do you doubt my having absolute control of myself to bear whatever they put on me to bear, and hold firmly to my will to overcome them! Oh! no delays."

"Yes!" she cried; "yes, there must be."

"You say it?"

The courage to repeat her cry was wanting.

She trembled visibly: she could more readily have bidden him bear her hence than have named a day for the interview with her parents; but desperately she feared that he would be the one to bid; and he had this of the character of destiny about him, that she felt in him a maker of facts. He was her dream in human shape, her eagle of men, and she felt like a lamb in the air; she had no resistance, only terror of his power, and a crushing new view of the nature of reality.

"I see!" said he, and his breast fell. Her timid inability to join with him for instant action reminded him that he carried many weights: a bad name among her people and class, and chains in private. He was old enough to strangle his impulses, if necessary, or any of the brood less fiery than the junction of his passions. "Well, well!—but we might so soon have broken through the hedge into the broad high-road! It is but to determine to do it—to take the bold short path instead of the wearisome circuit. Just a little lightning in the brain and tightening of the heart. Battles are won in that way: not by tender girls! and she is a girl, and the task is too much for her. So, then, we are in your hands, child! Adieu, and let the gold-crested serpent glide to her bed, and sleep, dream, and wake, and ask herself in the morning whether she is not a wedded soul. Is she not a serpent? gold-crested, all the world may see; and with a mortal bite, I know. I have had the bite before the kisses. That is rather an unjust reversal of the order of things. A propos, Hamlet was poisoned — ghost-poisoned."

"Mad, he was mad!" said Clotilde, recovering and smiling.

"He was born bilious; he partook of the father's constitution, not the mother's. High-thoughted, quick-nerved to follow the thought, reflective, if an interval yawned between his hand and the act, he was by nature two-minded: as full of conscience as a nursing mother that sleeps beside her infant: — she hears the silent beginning of a cry. Before the ghost walked he was an elementary hero; one puff of action would have whiffed away his melancholy. After it, he was a dizzy moralizer, waiting for the winds to blow him to his deed — or out. The apparition of his father to him poisoned a sluggish run of blood, and that venom in the blood distracted a head steeped in Wittenberg philosophy. With metaphysics in one and poison in the other, with the outer world opened on him and this world stirred to confusion, he wore the semblance of madness; he was throughout sane; sick, but never with his reason dethroned."

"Nothing but madness excuses his conduct to Ophelia!"

"Poison in the blood is a pretty good apology for infidelity to a lady."

"No!"

"Well, to an Ophelia of fifty?" said Alvan.

Clotilde laughed, not perfectly assured of the wherefore, but pleased to be able to laugh. Her friends were standing at the house door, farewells were spoken, Alvan had gone. And then she thought of the person that Ophelia of fifty might be, who would have to find a good apology for him in his dose of snake-bite, or love of a younger woman whom he termed gold-crested serpent.

He was a lover, surely a lover: he slid off to some chance bit of likeness to himself in every subject he discussed with her.

And she? She speeded recklessly on the back of the centaur when he had returned to the state of phantom, and the realities he threatened her with were no longer imminent.

## CHAPTER V.

CLOTILDE was of the order of the erring who should by rights have a short sermon to preface an exposure of them, administering the whip to her own sex and to ours, lest we scorn too much to take an interest in her. The exposure she has done for herself, and she has not had the art to frame her apology. The day after her meeting with her eagle, Alvan, she saw Prince Marko. She was gentle to him, in anticipation of his grief; she could hardly be ungentle on account of his obsequious beauty, and when her soft eyes and voice had thrilled him to an acute sensibility to the blow, honourably she inflicted it.

"Marko, my friend, you know that I cannot be false; then let me tell you I yesterday met the man who has but to lift his hand and I go to him, and he may lead me whither he will."

The burning eyes of her Indian Bacchus fixed on her till their brightness moistened and flashed.

Whatever was for her happiness he bowed his head to, he said. He knew the man.

Her duty was thus performed: she had plighted herself. For the first few days she was in dread of meeting, seeing, or hearing of Alvan. She feared the mention of a name that rolled the world so swiftly. Her parents had postponed their coming, she had no reason for instant alarm; it was his violent earnestness, his imperial self-confidence that she feared, as nervous people shrink from cannon: and neither meeting, seeing, nor hearing of him, she began to yearn, like the child whose curiosity is refreshed by a desire to try again the startling thing which frightened it. Her yearning grew, the illusion of her courage flooded back; she hoped he would present himself to claim her, marvelled that he did not, reproached him; she could almost have scorned him for listening to the hesitations of the despicable girl so little resembling what she really was — a poor untried girl, anxious only on behalf of her family to spare them a sudden shock. Remembering her generous considerations in their interests, she thought he should have known that the creature he called a child would have yielded upon supplication to fly with him. Her considerateness for him too, it struck her next, was the cause of her seeming cowardly, and the man ought to have perceived it and put it aside. He should have seen that she could be brave, and was a mate for him. And if his shallow experience of her wrote her down nerveless, his love should be doing.

Was it love? Her restoration to the belief in her possessing a decided will whispered of high achievements *she* could do in proof of love, had she the freedom of a man. She would not have listened (it was quite true) to a silly supplicating girl; she would not have allowed an interval to yawn after the first wild wooing of her. Prince Marko loved. Yes, that was love! It failed in no sign of the passion. She set herself to study it in Marko, and was moved by many sentiments, numbering among them pity, thankfulness, and the shiver of a feeling between admiration and pathetic esteem, like that the musician has for a precious instrument giving sweet sound when shattered. He served her faithfully, in spite of his distaste for some of his lady's commissions. She had to get her news of Alvan through Marko. He brought her particulars of the old trial of Alvan, and Alvan's oration in defence of himself for a lawless act of devotion to the baroness; nothing less than the successfully scheming to wrest by force from that lady's enemy a document precious to her lawful interests. It was one of those cases which have a really high gallant side as well as a bad; an excellent case for rhetoric. Marko supplied the world's opinion of the affair, bravely owning it to be not unfavourable. Her worthy relatives, the Frau v. Crestow and husband, had very properly furnished a report to the family of the memorable evening; and the hubbub over it, with the epithets applied to Alvan, intimated how he would have been received on a visit to demand her in marriage. There was no chance of her being allowed to enter houses where this "raging demagogue and popular buffoon" was a guest; his name was banished from her hearing, so she was compelled to have recourse to Marko. Unable to take such services without rewarding him, she fondled: it pained her to see him suffer. Those who toss crumbs to their domestic favourites will now and then be moved to toss meat, which is not so good for them, but the dumb mendicant's delight in it is winning, and a little cannot hurt. Besides, if any one had a claim on her it was the prince; and as he was always adoring, never importunate, he restored her to the pedestal she had been really rudely shaken from by that other who had caught her up suddenly into the air, and dropped her! A hand abandoned to her slave rewarded him immeasurably. A heightening of the reward almost took his life. In the peacefulness of dealing with a submissive love that made her queenly, the royal, which plucked her from throne to footstool, seemed predatory and insolent. Thus, after that scene of "first love," in which she had been actress, she became almost (with an inward thrill or two for the recovering of him) reconciled to the not seeing of the noble actor; for nothing could erase the scene — it was historic; and Alvan would always be thought of as a delicious electricity. She and Marko were together on the summer excursion of her people, and quite sisterly, she could say, in her delicate scorn of his advantages and her emotions. True gentlemen are imperfectly valued when they are under the shadow of giants; but still Clotilde's experience of a giant's manners was favourable to the liberty she could enjoy in a sisterly intimacy of this kind, rather warmer than her word for it would imply. She owned that she could better live the poetic life — that is, trifle with fire and reflect on its charms — in the society of Marko. He was very young, he was little more than an adolescent, and safely timid; a turn of her fingers would string or slacken him. One could play on him securely, thinking of a distant day — and some shipwreck of herself for an interlude — when he might be made happy.

Her strangest mood of the tender cruelty was when the passion to anatomize him beset her. The ground of it was, that she found him in her likeness, adoring as she adored, and a similar loftiness; now grovelling, now soaring; the most radiant of beings, the most abject; and the pleasure she had of the sensational comparison was in an alteregoistic home she found in him, that allowed of her gathering a picked self-knowledge, and of her saying: "That is like me: that is very like me: that is terribly like:" up to the point where the comparison wooed her no longer with an agreeable lure of affinity, but nipped her so shrewdly as to force her to say: "That is he, not I:" and the vivisected youth received the caress which quickened him to wholeness at a touch. It was given with impulsive tenderness, in pity of him. Anatomy is the title for the operation, because the probing of herself in another, with the liberty to cease probing as soon as it hurt her, allowed her while unhurt to feel that she prosecuted her researches in a dead body. The moment her strong susceptibility to the likeness shrank under a stroke of pain, she abstained from carving, and simultaneously conscious that he lived, she was kind to him.

"This love of yours, Marko — is it so deep?"

"I love you."

"You think me the highest and best?"

"You are."

"So deep that you could bear anything from me?"

"Try me!"

"Unfaithfulness?"

"You would be you!"

"Do you not say that because you cannot suspect evil of me?"

"Let me only see you!"

"You are sure that happiness would not smother it?"

"Has it done so yet?"

"Though you know I am a serpent to that man's music?"

"Ah, heaven! Oh! — do not say music. Yes! though anything!"

"And if ever you were to witness the power of his just breathing to me?"

"I would. . . . Ah!"

"What? If you saw his music working the spell? — even the first notes of his prelude!"

"I would wait."

"It might be for long."

"I would eat my heart."

"Bitter! bitter!"

"I would wait till he flung you off, and kneel to you."

She had a seizure of the nerves.

The likeness between them was, she felt, too flamingly keen to be looked at further. She reached to the dim idea of some such nauseous devotion, and took a shot in her breast as she did so, and abjured it, and softened to her victim. Clotilde opened her arms, charming away her wound, as she soothed him, both by the act of soothing and the reflection that she could not be so very like one whom she pitied and consoled.

She was charitably tender. If it be thought that she was cruel to excess, plead for her the temptation to simple human nature at sight of a youth who could be precipitated into the writhings of dissolution, and raised out of it by a smile. This young man's responsive spirit acted on her as the discovery of specifics for restoring soundness to the frame excites the brilliant empiric: he would slay us with benevolent soul to show the miracle of our revival. Worship provokes the mortal goddess to a manifestation of her powers; and really the devotee is full half to blame.

She had latterly been thinking of Alvan's rejection of the part of centaur; and his phrase, *the quadruped man*, breathed meaning. He was to gain her lawfully after dominating her utterly. That was right, but it levelled imagination. There is in the sentimental kingdom of Love a form of reasoning, by which a lady of romantic notions who is dominated utterly, will ask herself why she should be gained lawfully: and she is moved to do so by the consideration that if the latter, no necessity can exist for the former: and the reverse. In the union of the two conditions she sees herself slavishly domesticated.

With her Indian Bacchus imagination rose, for he was pliant: she had only to fancy, and he was beside her. — Quick to the saddle, away! The forest of terrors is ahead; they are at the verge of it; a last hamlet perches on its borders; the dwellers have haunted faces; the timbers of their huts lean to an upright in wry splinters; warnings are moaned by men and women with the voice of a night-wind; but on and on! the forest cannot be worse than a world defied. They drain a cup of milk apiece and they spur, for this is the way to the golden Indian land of the planted vine and the lover's godship. — Ludicrous! There is no getting farther than the cup of milk with Marko. They curvet and caper to be forward unavailingly. It should be Alvan to bring her through the forest to the planted vine in sunland. Her splendid prose Alvan could do what the sprig of poetry can but suggest. Never would malicious fairy in old woman's form have offered Alvan a cup of milk to paralyze his bride's imagination of him confronting perils. Yet, O shameful contrariety of the fates! he who could, will not; he who would, is incapable. Let it not be supposed that the desire of her bosom was to be run away with in person. Her simple human nature wished for the hero to lift her insensibly over the difficult opening chapter of the romance — through "the forest," or half imagined: that done, she felt bold enough to meet the unimagined, which, as there was no picture of it to terrify her, seemed an easy gallop into sunland. — Yes, but in the grasp of a great prose giant, with the poetic departed! Naturally she turned to caress the poetic while she had it beside her. And it was a wonder to observe the young prince's heavenly sensitiveness to every variation of her moods. He knew without hearing when she had next seen Alvan, though it had not been to speak to him. He looked, and he knew. The liquid darkness of his large eastern eyes cast a light that brought her heart out: she confessed it, and she comforted him. The sweetest in the woman caused her double-dealing.

Now she was aware that Alvan moved behind the screen concealing him. A common friend of Alvan and her family talked to her of him. He was an eminent professor, a middle-aged, grave and honourable man, not ignorant that her family entertained views opposed to the pretensions of such a man as the demagogue and Jew. Nevertheless Alvan could persuade him to abet the scheme for his meeting Clotilde; nay, to lead to it; ultimately to allow his own house to be their place of meeting. Alvan achieved the first of the steps unassisted. Whether or not his character stood well with a man of the world, his force of character, backed by solid attainments in addition to brilliant gifts, could win a reputable citizen and erudite to support him. Rhetoric in a worthy cause has good chances of carrying the gravest, and the cause might reasonably seem excellent to the professor when one promising fair to be the political genius of his time, but hitherto not the quietest of livers, could make him believe that marriage with this girl would be his clear salvation. The second step was undesignedly Clotilde's.

She was on the professor's arm at one of the great winter balls of her conductor's brethren in the law, and he said: "Alvan is here." She answered: "No, he has not yet come." — How could she tell that he was not present in the crowd?

"Has he come now?" said the professor.

"No."

And no Alvan was discernible.

"Now?"

"Not yet."

The professor stared about. She waited.

"*Now* he has come; he is in the room now," said Clotilde.

Alvan was perceived. He stood in the centre of the throng surrounding him to buzz about some recent pamphlet.

She could well play at faith in his magnetization of her, for as by degrees she made herself more nervously apprehensive by thinking of him, it came to an overclouding and then a panic; and that she took for the physical sign of his presence, and by that time, the hour being late, Alvan happened to have arrived. The touch of his hand, the instant naturalness in their speaking together after a long separation, as if there had not been an interval, confirmed her notion of his influence on her, almost to the making it planetary. And a glance at the professor revealed how picturesque it was. Alvan and he murmured aside. They spoke of it. What wonder that Alvan, though he saw Prince Marko whirl her in the dance, and keep her to the measure — dancing like a song of the limbs in his desperate poor lover's little flitting eternity of the possession of her — should say, after she had been led back to her friends: "That is he, then! one of the dragons guarding my apple of the Hesperides, whom I must brush away."

"He?" replied Clotilde, sincerely feeling Marko to be of as fractional a weight as her tone declared him. "Oh, he is my mute, harmless, he does not count among the dragons."

But there had been, notwithstanding the high presumption of his remark, a manful thickness of voice in Alvan's "That is he!" The rivals had fastened a look on one another, wary, strong, and summary as the wrestlers' first grapple. In fire of gaze, Marko was not outdone.

"He does not count? With those eyes of his?" Alvan exclaimed. He knew something of the sex, and spied from that point of knowledge into the character of Clotilde; not too venturesomely, with the assistance of rumour, hazarding the suspicion which he put forth as a certainty, and made sharply bitter to himself in proportion to the belief in it that his vehemence engendered: "I know all — without exception — all, everything; all! I repeat. But what of it, if I win you? as I shall — only aid me a little."

She slightly surprised the man by not striving to attenuate the import of the big and surcharged All: but her silence bore witness to his penetrative knowledge. Dozens of amorous gentlemen, lovers, of excellent substance, have before now prepared this peculiar dose for themselves — the dose of the lady silent under a sort of pardoning grand accusation; and they have had to drink it, and they have blinked over the tonic draught with such power of taking a bracing as their constitutions could summon. At no moment of their quaint mutual history are the sexes to be seen standing more acutely divided. Well may the lady be silent; her little sins are magnified to herself to the proportion of the greatness of heart forgiving her; and that, with his mysterious penetration and a throb of her conscience, holds her tongue-tied. She does not imagine the effect of her silence upon the magnanimous wretch. Some of these lovers, it has to be stated in sadness for the good name of man, have not preserved an attitude that said so nobly, "Child, thou art human — thou art woman!" They have undone it and gone to pieces with an injured lover's babble of persecuting inquiries for confessions. Some, on the contrary, retaining the attitude, have been unable to digest the tonic; they did not prepare their systems as they did their dose, possibly thinking the latter a supererogatory heavy thump on a trifle, the which was performed by them artfully for a means of swallowing and getting that obnoxious trifle well down. These are ever after love's dyspeptics. Very few indeed continue at heart in harmony with their opening note to the silent fair, because in truth the general anticipation is of her proclaiming, if not angelical innocence, a softly reddened or blush-rose of it, where the little guiltiness lies pathetic on its bed of white.

Alvan's robustness of temper, as a conqueror pleased with his capture, could inspirit him to feel as he said it: "I know all; what matters that to me?" Even her silence, extending the "all" beyond limits, as it did to the over-knowing man, who could number these indicative characteristics of the young woman: *impulsive, without will, readily able to lie:* her silence worked no discord in him. He would have remarked, that he was not looking out for a saint, but rather for a sprightly comrade, perfectly feminine, thoroughly mastered, young, graceful, comely, and a lady of station. Once in his good keeping, her lord would answer for her. And this was a manfully generous view of the situation. It belongs to the robustness of the conqueror's mood. But how of his opinion of her character in the fret of a baffling, a repulse, a defeat? Supposing the circumstances not to have helped her to shine as a heroine, while he was reduced to appear no hero to himself! Wise are the mothers who keep vigilant personal watch over their girls, were it only to guard them at present from the gentleman's condescending generosity, until he has become something more than robust in his ideas of the sex — say, for lack of the ringing word, fraternal.

Clotilde never knew, and Alvan would have been unable to date, the origin of the black thing flung at her in time to come — when the man was frenzied, doubtless, but it was in his mind, and more than froth of madness.

After the night of the ball they met beneath the sanctioning roof of the amiable professor; and on one occasion the latter, perhaps waxing anxious, and after bringing about the introduction of Clotilde to the sister of Alvan, pursued his prudent measures by passing the pair through a demi-ceremony of betrothal. It sprang Clotilde a stride nearer to reality, both actually and in feeling; and she began to show the change at home. A rebuff that came of the coupling of her name with Alvan's pushed her back as far below the surface as she had ever been. She waited for him to take the step she had again implored him not yet to take; she feared that he would, she marvelled at his abstaining; the old wheel revolved, as it ever does with creatures that wait for circumstances to bring the change they cannot work for themselves; and once more the two fell asunder. She had thoughts of the cloister. Her venerable relative died joining her hand to Prince Marko's; she was induced to think of marriage. An illness laid her prostrate; she contemplated the peace of death.

Shortly before she fell sick the prince was a guest of her father's, and had won the household by his perfect amiability as an associate. The grace and glow, and some of the imaginable accomplishments of an Indian Bacchus were native to him. In her convalescence, she asked herself what more she could crave than the worship of a godlike youth, whom she in return might cherish, strengthening his frail health with happiness. For she had seen how suffering ate him up; he required no teaching in the Spartan virtue of suffering, wolf-gnawed, silently. But he was a flower in sunshine to happiness, and he looked to her for it. Why should she withhold from him a thing so easily given? The convalescent is receptive and undesiring, or but very faintly desiring: the new blood coming into the frame like first dawn of light has not stirred the old passions; it is infant nature, with a tinge of superadded knowledge that is not cloud across it and lends it only a tender wistfulness.

Her physician sentenced her to the Alps, whither a friend, a daughter of our island, whose acquaintance she had made in Italy, was going, and at an invitation Clotilde accompanied her, and she breathed Alpine air. Marko sank into the category of dreams during sickness. There came a letter from the professor mentioning that Alvan was on one of the kingly Alpine heights in view, and the new blood running through her veins became a torrent. He there! So near! Could he not be reached?

He had a saying: *Two wishes make a will.*

The wishes of two lovers, he meant. A prettier sentence for lovers, and one more intoxicating to them, was never devised. It chirrups of the dear silly couple. Well, this was her wish. Was it his? Young health on the flow of her leaping blood cried out that it could not be other than Alvan's wish; she believed in his wishing it. Then as he wished and she wished, she had the will immediately, and it was all the more her own for being his as well. She hurried her friend and her friend's friends on horseback off to the heights where the wounded eagle lodged overlooking mountain and lake. The professor reported him outwearied with excess of work. Alvan lived the lives of three; the sins of thirty were laid to his charge. Do you judge of heroes as of lesser men? Her reckless defence of him, half spoken, half in her mind, helped her to comprehend his dealings with her, and how it was that he stormed her and consented to be beaten. He had a thousand occupations, an ambition out of the world of love, chains to break, temptations, leanings . . . tut, tut! She had not lived in her circle of society, and listened to the tales of his friends and enemies, and been the correspondent of flattering and flattered men of learning, without understanding how a man like Alvan found diversions when forbidden to act in a given direction: and now that her healthful new blood inspired the courage to turn two wishes to a will, she saw both herself and him **very** clearly, enough at least to pardon the man more than she did herself. She had perforce of her radiant new healthfulness arrived at an exact understanding of him. Where she was deluded was in supposing that she would no longer dread his impetuous disposition to turn rosy visions into facts. But she had the revived convalescent's ardour to embrace things positive while they were not knocking at the door; dreams were abhorrent to her, tasteless and innutritious; she cast herself on the flood, relying on his towering strength and mastery of men and events to bring her to some safe landing — the dream of hearts athirst for facts.

## CHAPTER VI.

ALVAN was at his writing-table doing stout gladiator's work on paper in a chamber of one of the gaunt hotels of the heights, which are Death's Heads there in Winter and have the tongues in summer, when a Swiss lad entered with a round grin to tell him that a lady on horseback below had asked for him — Dr. Alvan. Who could the lady be? He thought of too many. The thought of Clotilde was dismissed in its dimness. Issuing and beholding her, his face became illuminated as by a stroke of sunlight.

"Clotilde! by all the holiest!"

She smiled demurely, and they greeted.

She admired the look of rich pleasure shining through surprise in him. Her heart thanked him for appearing so handsome before her friends.

"I was writing," said he. "Guess to whom? — I had just finished my political stuff, and fell on a letter to the professor and another for an immediate introduction to your father."

"True?"

"The truth, as you shall see. So, you have come, you have found me! This time if I let you slip, may I be stamped slack-fingered."

"'Two wishes make a will,' you say."

He answered her with one of his bursts of brightness.

Her having sought him, he read for the frank surrender

which he was ready to match with a loyal devotion to his
captive. Her coming cleared everything.

Clotilde introduced him to her friends, and he was
enrolled a member of the party. His appearance was that
of a man to whom the sphinx has whispered. They
ascended to the topmost of the mountain stages, to another
caravanserai of tourists, whence the singular people emerge
in morning darkness nightcapped and blanketed, and
behold the great orb of day at his birth — he them.

Walking slowly beside Clotilde on the mountain way,
Alvan said: "Two wishes! Mine was in your breast.
You wedded yours to it. At last! — and we are one. Not
a word more of time lost. My wish is almost a will in
itself — was it not? — and has been wooing yours all this
while! — till the sleeper awakened, the well-spring leapt
up from the earth; and our two wishes united dare the
world to divide them. What can? My wish was your
destiny, yours is mine. We are one." He poetized on
his passion, and dramatized it: "Stood you at the altar,
I would pluck you from the man holding your hand! There
is no escape for you. Nay, into the vaults, were you to
grow pale and need my vital warmth — down to the vaults!
Speak — or no: look! That will do. You hold a Titan
in your eyes, like metal in the furnace, to turn him to any
shape you please, liquid or solid. You make him a god:
he is the river Alvan or the rock Alvan: but fixed or flowing, he is lord of you. That is the universal penalty: you
must, if you have this creative soul, be the slave of your
creature: if you raise him to heaven, you must be his!
Ay, look! I know the eyes! They can melt granite, they
can freeze fire. Pierce me, sweet eyes! And now flutter,
for there is that in me to make them."

"Consider!" Clotilde flutteringly entreated him.

"The world? you dear heaven of me! Looking down on
me does not compromise you, and I am not ashamed of my
devotions. I sat in gloom: you came: I saw my goddess
and worshipped. The world, Lutèce, the world is a
variable monster; it rends the weak whether sincere or
false; but those who weld strength with sincerity may
practise their rites of religion publicly, and it fawns to
them, and bellows to imitate. Nay, I say that **strength in**

love is the sole sincerity, and the world knows it, snuffs it in the air about us, and so we two are privileged. Politically also we know that strength is the one reality: the rest is shadow. Behind the veil of our human conventions power is constant as ever, and to perceive the fact is to have the divining rod — to walk clear of shams. He is the teacher who shows where power exists: he is the leader who wakens and forms it. Why have I unfailingly succeeded? — I never doubted! The world voluntarily opens a path to those who step determinedly. You — to your honour? — I won't decide — but you have the longest in my experience resisted. I have a Durandal to hew the mountain walls; I have a voice for ears, a net for butterflies, a hook for fish, and desperation to plunge into marshes: but the *feu follet* will not be caught. One must wait — wait till her desire to have a soul bids her come to us. She has come! A soul is hers: and see how, instantly, the old monster, the world, which has no soul — not yet: we are helping it to get one — becomes a shadow, powerless to stop or overawe. For I do give you a soul, think as you will of it. I give you strength to realize, courage to act. It is the soul that does things in this life — the rest is vapour. How do we distinguish love? — as we do music: by the pure note won from resolute strings. The tense chord is music, and it is love. This higher and higher mountain air, with you beside me, sweeps me like a harp."

"Oh! talk on, talk on! talk ever! do not cease talking to me!" exclaimed Clotilde.

"You feel the mountain spirit?"

"I feel that you reveal it."

"Tell me the books you have been reading."

"Oh, light literature — poor stuff."

"When we two read together you will not say that. Light literature is the garden and the orchard, the fountain, the rainbow, the far view; the view within us as well as without. Our blood runs through it, our history in the quick. The Philistine detests it, because he has no view, out or in. The dry confess they are cut off from the living tree, peeled and sapless, when they condemn it. The vulgar demand to have their pleasures in their own likeness — and let them swamp their troughs! they shall not degrade the fame of noble fiction. We are the choice public, which will have good writing for light reading. Poet, novelist, essayist, dramatist, shall be ranked honourable in my Republic. I am neither, but a man of law, a student of the sciences, a politician, on the road to government and statecraft: and yet I say I have learnt as much from light literature as from heavy — as much, that is, from the pictures of our human blood in motion as from the clever assortment of our forefatherly heaps of bones. Shun those who cry out against fiction and have no taste for elegant writing. For to have no sympathy with the playful mind is not to have a mind: it is a test. But name the books."

She named one or two.

"And when does Dr. Alvan date the first year of his Republic?"

"Clotilde!" he turned on her.

"My good sir?"

"These worthy good people who are with you: tell me — to-morrow we leave them!"

"Leave them?"

"You with me. No more partings. The first year, the first day shall be dated from to-morrow. You and I proclaim our Republic on these heights. All the ceremonies to follow. We will have a reaping of them, and make a sheaf to present to the world with compliments. To-morrow!"

"You do not speak seriously?"

"I jest as little as the Talmud. Decide at once, in the happy flush of this moment."

"I cannot listen to you, dear sir!"

"But your heart beats!"

"I am not mistress of it."

"Call me master of it. I make ready for to-morrow."

"No! no! no! A thousand times no! You have been reading too much fiction and verse. Properly I should spurn you."

"Will you fail me, play *feu follet*, ward me off again?"

"I must be won by rules, brave knight!"

"Will you be won?"

"And are you he — the Alvan who would not be centaur?"

"I am he who chased a marsh-fire, and encountered a retiarius, and the meshes are on my head and arms. I fancied I dealt with a woman; a woman needing protection! She has me fast — I am netted, centaur or man. That is between us two. But think of us facing the world, and trust me; take my hand, take the leap; I am the best fighter in that fight. Trust it to me, and all your difficulties are at an end. To fly solves the problem."

"Indeed, indeed, I have more courage than I had," said Clotilde.

His eyes dilated, steadied, speculated, weighed her.

"Put it to proof while you can believe in it!"

"How is it every one but you thinks me bold?" she complained.

"Because I carry a touchstone that brings out the truth. I am your reality: all others are phantoms. You can impose on them, not on me. Courage for one inspired plunge you may have, and it will be your salvation: — southward, over to Italy, that is the line of flight, and the subsequent struggle will be mine: you will not have to face it. But the courage for daily contention at home, standing alone, while I am distant and maligned — can you fancy your having that? No! be wise of what you really are; cast the die for love, and mount away to-morrow."

"Then," said Clotilde, with elvish cunning, "do you doubt your ability to win me without a scandal?"

"Back me, and I win you!" he replied in a tone of unwonted humility: a sudden droop.

She let her hand fall. He grasped it.

"Gradations appear to be unknown to you," she said.

He cried out: "Count the years of life, span them, think of the work to be done, and ask yourself whether time and strength should run to waste in retarding the inevitable? Pottering up steps that can be taken at one bound is very well for peasant pilgrims whose shrine is their bourne, and their kneecaps the footing stumps. But for us two life begins up there. Onward, and everywhere around, when we two are together, is our shrine. I have worked, and wasted life; I have not lived, and I thirst to live."

She murmured, in a fervour, "You shall!" and slipped behind her defences. "To-morrow morning we shall wander about; I must have a little time; all to-morrow morning we can discuss plans."

"You know you command me," said he, and gazed at her.

She was really a child compared with him in years, and if it was an excuse for taking her destiny into his hands, she consenting, it was also a reason why he dared not press his whole weight to win her to the step.

She had the pride of the secret knowledge of her command of this giant at the long table of the guests at dinner, where, after some play of knife and fork among notable professors, Prussian officers, lively Frenchmen and Italians, and the usual over-supply of touring English of both sexes, not encouraging to conversation in their look of pallid disgust of the art, Alvan started general topics and led them. The lead came to him naturally, because he was a natural speaker, of a mind both stored and effervescent; and he was genial, interested in every growth of life. She did not wonder at his popularity among men of all classes and sets, or that he should be famed for charming women. Her friend was enraptured with him. Friendly questions pressed in an evening chatter between the ladies, and Clotilde fenced, which is half a confession.

"But are you not engaged?" said the blunt English-woman.

According to the explanation, Clotilde was hardly engaged. It was not an easy thing to say how she stood definitely. She had obeyed her dying relative and dearest on earth by joining her hand to Prince Marko's, and had pleased her parents by following it up with the kindest attentions to the prince. It had been done, however, for the sake of peace; and chiefly for his well-being. She had reserved her *full* consent: the plighting was incomplete. Prince Marko knew that there was another, a magical person, a genius of the ring, irresistible. He had been warned, that should the other come forth to claim her. . . . And she was about to write to him this very night to tell him . . . tell him fully. . . . In truth, she loved both, but each so differently! And both loved her! And she had to make her choice of one, and tell the prince she did love him, but . . . Dots are the best of symbols for rendering cardisophistical subtleties intelligible, and as they are much used in dialogue, one should have now and then permission to print them. Especially feminine dialogue referring to matters of the uncertain heart takes assistance from troops of dots; and not to understand them at least as well as words, when words have as it were conducted us to the brink of expression, and shown us the precipice, is to be dull, bucolic of the marketplace.

Sunless rose the morning. The blanketed figures went out to salute a blanketed sky. Drizzling they returned, images of woefulness in various forms, including laughter's. Alvan frankly declared himself the disappointed showman; he had hoped for his beloved to see the sight long loved by him of golden chariot and sun-steeds crossing the peaks and the lakes; and his disappointment became consternation on hearing Clotilde's English friend (after objection to his pagan clothing of the solemn reality of sunrise, which destroyed or minimized by too materially defining a grandeur that derived its essence from mystery, she thought) announce the hour for her departure. He promised her a positive sunrise if she would delay. Her child lay recovering from an illness in the town below, and she could not stay. But Clotilde had coughed in the damp morning air, and it would, he urged, be dangerous for her to be exposed to it. Had not the lady heard her cough? She had, but personally she was obliged to go; with her child lying ill she could not remain. "But, madam, do you hear that cough again? Will you drag her out with such a cough as that?" The lady repeated "My child!" Clotilde said it had been agreed they should descend this day; her friend must be beside her child. Alvan thundered an "Impossible!" The child was recovering; Clotilde was running into danger: he argued with the senseless woman, opposing reason to the feminine sentiment of the maternal, and of course he was beaten. He was compelled to sit and gnaw his eloquence. Clotilde likened his appearance to a strangled roar.

"Mothers and their children are too much for me!" he said, penitent for his betrayal of over-urgency, as he helped to wrap her warmly, and counselled her very mode of breathing in the raw mountain atmosphere.

"I admire you for knowing when to yield," said she.

He groaned, with frown and laugh: "You know what I would beg!"

She implored him to have some faith in her.

The missiles of the impassioned were discharged at the poor English: a customary volley in most places where they intrude after quitting their shores, if they diverge from the avenue of hotel-keepers and waiters: but Clotilde pointed out to him that her English friend was not showing coldness in devoting herself to her child.

"No, they attend to their duties," he assented generally, desperately just.

"And you owe it to her that you have seen me."

"I do," he said, and forthwith courted the lady to be forgiven.

Clotilde was taken from him in a heavy down-pour and trailing of mists.

At the foot of the mountain a boy handed her a letter from Alvan — a burning flood, rolled out of him like lava after they had separated on the second plateau, and confided to one who knew how to outstrip pathfarers. She entered her hotel across the lake, and met a telegram. At night the wires flashed "Sleep well" to her; on her awaking, "Good morning." A lengthened history of the day was telegraphed for her amusement. Again at night there was a "God guard you!"

"Who can resist him?" sighed Clotilde, excited, nervous, flattered, happy, but yearning to repose and be curtained from the buzz of the excess of life that he put about her. This time there was no prospect of his courtship relapsing.

"He is a wonderful, an ideal lover!" replied her friend.

"If he were only that!" said Clotilde, musing expressively. "If, dear Englishwoman, he were only that, he might be withstood. But Alvan mounts high over such lovers: he is a wonderful and ideal *man:* so great, so generous, heroical, giant-like, that what he wills must be."

The Englishwoman was quick enough to seize an indication difficult to miss — more was expected to be said of him.

"You see the perfect gentleman in Dr. Alvan," she remarked, for she had heard him ordering his morning bath at the hotel, and he had also been polite to her under vexation.

Clotilde nodded hurriedly; she saw something infinitely greater, and disliked the bringing of that island microscope to bear upon a giant. She found it repugnant to hear a word of Alvan as a perfect gentleman. Justly, however, she took him for a splendid nature, and assuming upon good authority that the greater contains the lesser, she supposed the lesser to be a chiselled figure serviceably alive in the embrace.

## CHAPTER VII.

He was down on the plains to her the second day, and as usual when they met, it was as if they had not parted; his animation made it seem so. He was like summer's morning sunlight, his warmth striking instantly through her blood dispersed any hesitating strangeness that sometimes gathers during absences, caused by girlish dread of a step to take, or shame at the step taken, when coldish gentlemen rather create these backflowings and gaps in the feelings. She had grown reconciled to the perturbation of his messages, and would have preferred to have him startling and thrilling her from a distance; but seeing him, she welcomed him, and feeling in his bright presence not the faintest chill of the fit of shyness, she took her bravery of heart for a sign that she had reached his level, and might own it by speaking of the practical measures to lead to their union. On one subject sure to be raised against him by her parents, she had a right to be inquisitive: the baroness.

She asked to see a photograph of her.

Alvan gave her one out of his pocketbook, and watched her eyelids in profile as she perused those features of the budless grey woman. The eyelids in such scrutinies reveal the critical mind; Clotilde's drooped till they almost closed upon their lashes — deadly criticism.

"Think of her age," said Alvan, colouring. He named a grandmaternal date for the year of the baroness's birth.

Her eyebrows now stood up; her contemplation of those disenchanting lineaments came to an abrupt finish.

She returned the square card to him, slowly shaking her head, still eyeing earth as her hand stretched forth the card laterally. He could not contest the woeful verdict.

"Twenty years back!" he murmured, writhing. The baroness was a woman fair to see in the days twenty years back, though Clotilde might think it incredible: she really was once.

Clotilde resumed her doleful shaking of the head; she sighed. He shrugged; she looked at him, and he blinked a little. For the first time since they had come together she had a clear advantage, and as it was likely to be a rare occasion, she did not let it slip. She sighed again. He was wounded by her underestimate of his ancient conquest.

"Yes — *now*," he said, impatiently.

"I cannot feel jealousy, I cannot feel rivalry," said she, sad of voice.

The humour of her tranced eyes in the shaking head provoked him to defend the baroness for her goodness of heart, her energy of brain.

Clotilde 'tolled' her naughty head.

"But it is a strong face," she said, "a strong face — a strong jaw, by Lavater! You were young — and daringly adventurous; she was captivating in her distress. Now she is old — and you are friends."

"Friends, yes," Alvan replied, and praised the girl, as of course she deserved to be praised for her open mind.

"We are friends!" he said, dropping a deep-chested breath. The title this girl scornfully supplied was balm to the vanity she had stung, and his burnt skin was too eager for a covering of any sort to examine the mood of the giver. She had positively humbled him so far as with a single word to relieve him; for he had seen bristling chapters in her look at the photograph. Yet for all the natural sensitiveness of the man's vanity, he did not seek to bury the subject at the cost of a misconception injurious in the slightest degree to the sentiments he entertained toward the older lady as well as the younger. "Friends! you are right; good friends; only you should know that it is just a little — a trifle different. The fact is, I cannot kill the past, and I would not. It would try me sharply to break the tie connecting us, were it possible to break it. I am bound to her by gratitude. She is old now; and were she twice that age, I should retain my feeling for her. You raise your eyes, Clotilde! Well, when I was much younger I found this lady in desperate ill-fortune, and she honoured me with her confidence. Young man though I was, I defended her; I stopped at no measure to defend her: against a powerful husband, remember — the most unscrupulous of foes, who sought to rob her of every right she possessed. And what I did then I again would do. I was vowed to her interests, to protect a woman shamefully wronged; I did not stick at trifles, as you know; you have read my speech in defence of myself before the court. By my interpretation of the case, I was justified; but I estranged my family and made the world my enemy. I gave my time and money, besides the forfeit of reputation, to the case, and reasonably there was an arrangement to repay me out of the estate reserved for her, so that the baroness should not be under the degradation of feeling herself indebted. You will not think that out of the way: men of the world do not. As for matters of the heart between us, we're as far apart as the Poles."

He spoke hurriedly. He had said all that could be expected of him.

They were in a wood, walking through lines of spruce firs of deep golden green in the yellow beams. One of these trees among its well-robed fellows fronting them was all lichen-smitten. From the low sweeping branches touching earth to the plumed top, the tree was dead-black as its shadow; a vision of blackness.

"I will compose a beautiful, dutiful, modest, oddest,

beseeching, screeching, mildish, childish epistle to her, and you shall read it, and if you approve it, we shall despatch it," said Clotilde.

"There speaks my gold-crested serpent at her wisest!" replied Alvan. "And now for my visit to your family: I follow you in a day. *En avant! contre les canons!* A run to Lake Leman brings us to them in the afternoon. I shall see you in the evening. So our separation won't be for long this time. All the auspices are good. We shall not be rich — nor poor."

Clotilde reminded him that a portion of money would be brought to the store by her.

"We don't count it," said he. "Not rich, certainly. And you will not expect me to make money by my pen. Above all things I detest the writing for money. Fiction and verse appeal to a besotted public, that judges of the merit of the work by the standard of its taste: — avaunt! And journalism for money is Egyptian bondage. No slavery is comparable to the chains of hired journalism. My pen is my fountain — the key of me; and I give myself, I do not sell. I write when I have matter in me and in the direction it presses for, otherwise not one word!"

"I would never ask you to sell yourself," said Clotilde. "I would rather be in want of common comforts."

He squeezed her wrist. They were again in front of the black-draped blighted tree. It was the sole tree of the host clad thus in scurf bearing a semblance of livid metal. They looked at it as having seen it before, and passed on.

"But the wife of Sigismund Alvan will not be poor in renown!" he resumed, radiating his full bloom on her.

"My highest ambition is to be Sigismund Alvan's wife!" she exclaimed.

To hear her was as good as wine, and his heart came out on a genial chuckle. "Ay, the choice you have made is not, by heaven, so bad. Sigismund Alvan's wife shall take the foremost place of all. Look at me." He lifted his head to the highest on his shoulders, widening his eagle eyes. He was now thoroughly restored and in his own upper element, expansive after the humiliating contraction of his man's vanity under the glances of a girl.

"Do you take me for one who *could* be content with the part of second? I will work and do battle unceasingly, but I will have too the prize of battle to clasp it, savour it richly. I was not fashioned to be the lean meek martyr of a cause, not I. I carry too decisive a weight in the balance to victory. I have a taste for fruits, my fairest! And Republics, my bright Lutetia, can give you splendid honours." He helped her to realize this with the assuring splendour of his eyes.

"'Bride of the Elect of the People!' is not that as glorious a title, think you, as queen of an hereditary sovereign mumbling of God's grace on his worm-eaten throne? I win that seat by service, by the dedication of this brain to the people's interests. They have been ground to the dust, and I lift them, as I did a persecuted lady in my boyhood. I am the soldier of justice against the army of the unjust. But I claim my reward. If I live to fight, I live also to enjoy. I will have my station. I win it not only because I serve, but because also I have seen, have seen ahead, seen where all is dark, read the unwritten — because I am soldier and prophet. The brain of man is Jove's eagle and his lightning on earth — the title to majesty henceforth. Ah! my fairest; entering the city beside me, and the people shouting around, she would not think her choice a bad one?"

Clotilde made sign and gave some earnest on his arm of ecstatic hugging.

"We may have hard battles, grim deceptions, to go through before that day comes," he continued after a while. "The day is coming, but we must wait for it. work on. I have the secret of how to head the people — to put a head to their movement and make it irresistible, as I believe it will be beneficent. I set them moving on the lines of the law of things. I am no empty theorizer, no phantasmal speculator; I am the man of science in politics. When my system is grasped by the people, there is but a step to the realization of it. One step. It will be taken in my time, or acknowledged later. I stand for index to the people of the path they should take to triumph — must take, as triumph they must sooner or later: not by the route of what is called Progress — pooh!

That is a middle-class invention to effect a compromise. With the people the matter rests — with their intelligence! meanwhile my star is bright and shines reflected."

"I notice," she said, favouring him with as much reflection as a splendid lover could crave for, "that you never look down, you never look on the ground, but always either up or straight before you."

"People have remarked it," said he, smiling. "Here we are at this funereal tree again. All roads lead to Rome, and ours appears to conduct us perpetually to this tree. It's the only dead one here."

He sighted the plumed black top and along the swelling branches decorously clothed in decay: a salted ebon moss when seen closely; the small grey particles giving a sick shimmer to the darkness of the mass. It was very witch-like, of a witch in her incantation-smoke.

"Not a single bare spot! but dead, dead as any peeled and fallen!" said Alvan, fingering a tuft of the sooty snake-lichen. "This is a tree for a melancholy poet — eh, Clotilde? — for him to come on it by moonlight, after a scene with his mistress, or tales of her! By the way and by the way, my fair darling, let me never think of your wearing this kind of garb for me, should I be ordered off the first to join the dusky army below. Women who put on their dead husbands in public are not well-mannered women, though they may be excellent professional widows, excellent!"

He snapped the lichen-dust from his fingers, observing that he was not sure the contrast of the flourishing and blighted was not more impressive in sunlight: and then he looked from the tree to his true love's hair. The tree at a little distance seemed run over with sunless lizards: her locks were golden serpents.

"Shall I soon see your baroness?" Clotilde asked him.

"Not in advance of the ceremony," he answered. "In good time. You understand — an old friend making room for a new one, and that one young and beautiful, with golden tresses; at first. . . ! But her heart is quite sound. Have no fear! I guarantee it; I know her to the roots. She desires my welfare, she does my behests. If I am bound to her by gratitude, so, and in a greater degree, is she to me. The utmost she will demand is that my bride shall be worthy of me — a good mate for me in the fight to come; and I have tested my bride and found her half my heart; therefore she passes the examination with the baroness."

They left the tree behind them.

"We will take good care not to return this way again," said Alvan, without looking back. "That tree belongs to a plantation of the under world; its fellows grow in the wood across Acheron, and that tree has looked into the ghastliness of the flood and seen itself. Hecate and Hermes know about it. Phœbus cannot light it. That tree stands for Death blooming. We think it sinister, but *down there* it is a homely tree. Down there! When do we go? The shudder in that tree is the air exchanging between Life and Death — the ghosts going and coming: it's on the border line. I just felt the creep. I think you did. The reason is — there is always a material reason — that you were warm, and a bit of chill breeze took you as you gazed, while for my part I was imagining at that very moment what of all possible causes *might* separate us, and I acknowledged that death could do the trick. But death, my love, is far from us two!"

"Does she look as grimmish as she does in the photograph?" said Clotilde.

"Who? the baroness?" Alvan laughed. The baroness was not so easily defended from a girl as from her husband, it appeared. "She is the best of comrades, best of friends. She has her faults; may not relish the writ announcing her final deposition, but be you true to me, and as true as she has unfailingly been to me, she will be to you. That I can promise. My poor Lucie! She is winter, if you will. It is not the winter of the steppes; you may compare her to winter in a noble country; a fine landscape of winter. The outlines of her face. . . . She has a great brain. How much I owe that woman for instruction! You meet now and then men who have the woman in them without being womanized; they are the pick of men. And the choicest women are those who yield not a feather of their womanliness for some amount of manlike strength. And she is one; man's brain, woman's heart. I thought her unique till I heard of you. And how do I stand between you two? She has the only fault you can charge me with; she is before me in time, as I am before you. Shall I spoil you as she spoilt me? No, no! Obedience to a boy is the recognition of the heir-apparent, and I respect the salique law as much as I love my love. I do not offer obedience to a girl, but succour, support. You will not rule me, but you will invigorate, and if you are petted, you shall not be spoilt. Do not expect me to show like that undertakerly tree till my years are one hundred. Even then it will be dangerous to repose beneath my branches in the belief that I am sapless because I have changed colour. We Jews have a lusty blood. We are strong of the earth. We serve you, but you must minister to us. Sensual? We have truly excellent appetites. And why not? Heroical too! Soldiers, poets, musicians; the Gentile's masters in mental arithmetic — keenest of weapons: surpassing him in common sense and capacity for brotherhood. Ay, and in charity; or what stores of vengeance should we not have nourished! Already we have the money-bags. Soon we shall hold the chief offices. And when the popular election is as unimpeded as the coursing of the blood in a healthy body, the Jew shall be foremost and topmost, for he is pre-eminently by comparison the brain of these latter-day communities. But that is only my answer to the brutish contempt of the Jew. I am no champion of a race. I am for the world, for man!"

Clotilde remarked that he had many friends, all men of eminence, and a large following among the people.

He assented: "Yes: Tresten, Retka, Kehlen, the Nizzian. Yes, if I were other than for legality: — if it came to a rising, I could tell off able lieutenants."

"Tell me of your interview with Ironsides," she said proudly and fondly.

"Would this ambitious little head know everything?" said Alvan, putting his lips among the locks. "Well, we met: he requested it. We agreed that we were on neutral ground for the moment: that he might ultimately have to decapitate me, or I to banish him, but temporarily we could compare our plans for governing. He showed me his hand. I showed him mine. We played open-handed, like two at whist. He did not doubt my honesty, and I astonished him by taking him quite in earnest. He has dealt with diplomatists, who imagine nothing but shuffling: the old Ironer! I love him for his love of common sense, his contempt of mean deceit. He will outwit you, but his dexterity is a giant's — a simple evolution rapidly performed: and nothing so much perplexes pygmies! Then he has them, bagsful of them! The world will see; and see giant meet giant, I suspect. He and I proposed each of us in the mildest manner contrary schemes — schemes to stiffen the hair of Europe! Enough that we parted with mutual respect. He is a fine fellow: and so was my friend the Emperor Tiberius, and so was Richelieu. Napoleon was a fine engine: — there is a difference. Yes, Ironsides is a fine fellow! but he and I may cross. His ideas are not many. The point to remember is that he is iron on them: he can drive them hard into the density of the globe. He has quick nerves and imagination: he can conjure up, penetrate, and traverse complications — an enemy's plans, all that the enemy will be able to combine, and the likeliest that he will do. Good. We opine that we are equal to the same. He is for kingcraft to mask his viziercraft — and save him the labour of patiently attempting oratory and persuasion, which accomplishment he does not possess: — it is not in iron. *We* think the more precious metal will beat him when the broader conflict comes. But such an adversary is not to be underrated. I do not underrate him: and certainly not he me. Had he been born with the gifts of patience and a fluent tongue, and not a petty noble, he might have been for the people, as knowing them the greater power. He sees that their knowledge of their power must eventually come to them. In the meantime his party is forcible enough to assure him he is not fighting a losing game at present: and he is, no doubt, by lineage and his traditions monarchical. He is curiously simple, not really cynical. His apparent cynicism is sheer irritability. His contemptuous phrases are directed against obstacles: against things, persons, nations that oppose him or cannot serve his turn: against his king, if his king is restive; but he respects his king: against your friends' country, because there is no fixing it to a line of policy, and it seems to have collapsed; but he likes that country the best in Europe after his own. He is nearest to contempt in his treatment of his dupes and tools, who are dropped out of his mind when he has quite squeezed them for his occasion; to be taken up again when they are of use to him. Hence he will have no following. But let me die to-morrow, the party I have created survives. In him you see the dam, in me the stream. Judge, then, which of them gains the future! — admitting that in the present he may beat me. He is a Prussian, stoutly defined from a German, and yet again a German stoutly defined from our borderers: and that completes him. He has as little the idea of humanity as the sword of our Hermann, the cannon-ball of our Frederick. Observe him. What an eye he has! I watched it as we were talking: — and he has, I repeat, imagination; he can project his mind in front of him as far as his reasoning on the possible allows: and that eye of his flashes; and not only flashes, you see it hurling a bolt; it gives me the picture of a Balearic slinger about to whizz the stone: for that eye looks far, and is hard, and is dead certain of its mark — within his practical compass, as I have said. I see farther, and I fancy I proved to *him* that I am not a dreamer. In my opinion, when we cross our swords I stand a fair chance of not being worsted. We shall: — you shrink? Figuratively, my darling — have no fear! Combative as we may be, both of us, we are now grave seniors, we have serious business: a party looks to him, my party looks to me. Never need you fear that I shall be at sword or pistol with any one. I will challenge my man, whoever he is that needs a lesson, to touch buttons on a waistcoat with the button on a foil, or drill fives and eights in cards at twenty paces: but I will not fight him though he offend me, for I am stronger than my temper, and as I do not want to take his nip of life, and judge it to be of less value than mine, the imperilling of either is an absurdity."

"Oh! because I know you are incapable of craven fear," cried Clotilde, answering aloud the question within herself of why she so much admired, why she so fondly loved him. To feel his courage backing his high good sense was to repose in security, and her knowledge that an astute self-control was behind his courage assured her he was invincible. It seemed to her, therefore, as they walked side by side, and she saw their triumphant pair of figures in her fancy, natural that she should instantly take the step to prepare her for becoming his Republican Princess. She walked an equal with the great of the earth, by virtue of her being the mate of the greatest of the great; she trod on some, and she thrilled gratefully to the man who sustained her and shielded her on that eminence. Elect of the people he! and by a vaster power than kings can summon through the trumpet! She could surely pass through the trial with her parents that she might step to the place beside him! She pressed his arm to be physically a sharer of his glory. Was it love? It was as lofty a stretch as her nature could strain to.

She named the city on the shores of the great Swiss lake where her parents were residing; she bade him follow her thither, and name the hotel where he was to be found, the hour when he was to arrive. "Am I not precise as an office clerk?" she said, with a pleasant taste of the reality her preciseness pictured.

"Practical as the head of a State department," said he, in good faith.

"I shall not keep you waiting," she resumed.

"The sooner we are together after the action opens the better for our success, my golden crest!"

"Have no misgiving, Sigismund. You have transformed me. A spark of you is in my blood. Come. I shall send word to your hotel when you are to appear. But you will come, you will be there, I know. I know you so entirely."

"As a rule, Lutetia, women know no more than half of a man even when they have married him. At least you ought to know me. You know that if I were to exercise my will firmly now — it would not waver if I called it forth — I could carry you off and spare you the flutter you will have to go through during our interlude with papa and mama."

"I almost wish you would," said she. She looked half imploringly, biting her lip to correct the peeping wish.

Alvan pressed a finger on one of her dimples: "Be brave. Flight and defiance are our last resource. Now that I see you resolved I shun the scandal, and we will leave it to them to insist on it, if it must be. How can you be less than resolved after I have poured my influence into your veins? The other day on the heights — had you consented then? Well! it would have been very well, but not so well. We two have a future, and are bound to make the opening chapters good sober reading, for an example, if we can. I take you from your father's house, from your mother's arms, from the 'God speed' of your friends. That is how Alvan's wife should be presented to the world."

Clotilde's epistle to the baroness was composed, approved, and despatched. To a frigid eye it read as more hypocritical than it really was; for supposing it had to be written, the language of the natural impulse called up to write it was necessarily in request, and that language is easily overdone, so as to be discordant with the situation, while it is, as the writer feels, a fairly true and well-formed expression of the pretty impulse. But wiser is it always that the star in the ascendant should not address the one waning. Hardly can a word be uttered without grossly wounding. She would not do it to a younger rival: the letter strikes on the recipient's age! She babbles of a friendship: she plays at childish ninny! The display of her ingenuous happiness causes feminine nature's bosom to rise in surges. The declarations of her devotedness to the man waken comparisons with a deeper, a longer-tried suffering. Actually the letter of the rising star assumes personal feeling to have died out of the abandoned luminary, and personal feeling is chafed to its acutest edge by the perusal; contempt also of one who can stupidly simulate such innocence, is roused.

Among Alvan's gifts the understanding of women did not rank high. He was too robust, he had been too successful. Your very successful hero regards them as ninepins destined to fall, the whole tuneful nine, at a peculiar poetical twist of the bowler's wrist, one knocking down the other — figuratively, for their scruples, or for their example with their sisters. His tastes had led him into the avenues of success, and as he had not encountered grand resistances, he entertained his opinion of their sex. The particular maxim he cherished was, to stake everything on his making a favourable first impression: after which single figure, he said, all your empty naughts count with women for hundreds, thousands, millions: noblest virtues are but sickly units. He would have stared like any Philistine at the tale of their capacity to advance to a likeness unto men in their fight with the world. Women for him were objects to be chased, the politician's relaxation, taken like the sportsman's business, with keen relish both for the pursuit and the prey, and a view of the termination of his pastime. Their feelings he could appreciate during the time when they flew and fell, perhaps a little longer; but the change in his own feelings withdrew him from the communion of sentiment. This is the state of men who frequent the avenues of success. At present he was thinking of a wife, and he approved the epistle to the baroness cordially.

"I do think it a nice kind of letter, and quite humble enough," said Clotilde.

He agreed, "Yes, yes: she knows already that this is really serious with me."

So much for the baroness.

Now for their parting. A parting that is no worse than the turning of a page to a final meeting is made light of, but felt. Reason is all in our favour, and yet the gods are jealous of the bliss of mortals; the slip between the cup and the lip is emotionally watched for, even though it be not apprehended, when the cup trembles for very fulness. Clotilde required reassuring and comforting: "I am certain you will prevail; you must; you cannot be resisted; I stand to witness to the fact," she sighed in a languor: "only, my people are hard to manage. I see more clearly now, that I have imposed on them; and they have given away by a sort of compact so long as I did nothing decisive. That I see. But, then again, have I not your spirit in me now? What has ever resisted you? — Then, as I am Alvan's wife, I share his heart with his fortunes, and I do not really dread the scenes from anticipating failure, still — the truth is, I fear I am three parts an actress, and the fourth feels itself a shivering morsel to face reality. No, I do not really feel it, but press my hand, I shall be true — I am so utterly yours: and because I have such faith in you. You never yet have failed."

"Never: and it is impossible for me to conceive it," said Alvan, thoughtfully.

His last word to her on her departure was "Courage!" Hers to him was conveyed by the fondest of looks. She had previously said "To-morrow!" to remind him of his appointment to be with her on the morrow, and herself that she would not long stand alone. She did not doubt of her courage while feasting on the beauty of one of the acknowledged strong men of earth. She kissed her hand, she flung her heart to him from the waving fingers.

## CHAPTER VIII

ALVAN, left to himself, had a quiet belief in the subjugation of his tricksy Clotilde, and the inspiriting he had given her. All the rest to come was mere business matter of the conflict, scarcely calling for a plan of action. Who can hold her back when a woman is decided to move? Husbands have tried it vainly, and parents; and though the husband and the parents are not dealing with the same kind of woman, you see the same elemental power in her under both conditions of rebel wife and rebel daughter to break conventional laws, and be splendidly irrational. That is, if she can be decided: in other words, aimed at a mark and inflamed to fly the barriers intercepting. He fancied he had achieved it. Alvan thanked his fortune that he had to treat with parents. The consolatory sensation of a pure intent soothed his inherent wildness, in the contemplation of the possibility that the latter might be roused by those people, her parents, to upset his honourable ambition to win a wife after the fashion of orderly citizens. It would be on their heads! But why vision mischance? An old half-jesting prophecy of his among his friends, that he would not pass his fortieth year, rose upon his recollection without casting a shadow. Lo, the reckless prophet about to marry! No dark bride, no skeleton, no colourless thing, no lichened tree, was she. Not Death, my friends, but Life, is the bride of this doomed fortieth year! Was animation ever vivider in contrast with obstruction? Her hair would kindle the frosty shades to a throb of vitality: it would be sunshine in the subterranean sphere. The very thinking of her dispersed that realm of the poison hue, and the eternally inviting phosphorescent, still, curved forefinger, which says, "Come."

To think of her as his vernal bride, while the snowy Alps were a celestial garden of no sunset before his eyes, was to have the taste of mortal life in the highest. He wondered how it was that he could have waited so long for her since the first night of their meeting, and he just distinguished the fact that he lived with the pulses of the minutes, much as she did, only more fierily. The ceaseless warfare called politics must have been the distraction: he forgot any other of another kind. He was a bridegroom for whom the rosed Alps rolled out a panorama of illimitable felicity. And there were certain things he must overcome before he could name his bride his own, so that his innate love of contention, which had been constantly flattered by triumph, brought his whole nature into play with the prospect of the morrow: not much liking it either. There is a nerve in brave warriors that does not like the battle before the crackle of musketry is heard, and the big artillery.

Methodically, according to his habit, he jotted down the hours of the trains, the hotel mentioned by Clotilde, the address of her father; he looked to his card-case, his writing materials, his notes upon Swiss law, considering that the scene would be in Switzerland, and he was a lawyer bent on acting within and up to the measure of the law as well as pleading eloquently. The desire to wing a telegram to her he thought it wise to repress, and he found himself in consequence composing verses, turgid enough, even to his own judgement. Poets would have failed at such a time, and he was not one, but an orator enamoured. He was a wild man, cased in the knowledge of jurisprudence, and wishing to enter the ranks of the soberly blissful. These he could imagine that he complimented by the wish. Then why should he doubt of his fortune? He did not.

The night passed, the morning came, and carried him on his journey. Late in the afternoon he alighted at the hotel he called Clotilde's. A letter was handed to him. His eyes all over the page caught the note of it for her beginning of the battle and despair at the first repulse. "And now my turn!" said he, not overjoyously. The words Jew and demagogue and baroness, quoted in the letter, were old missiles hurling again at him. But Clotilde's parents were yet to learn that this Jew, demagogue, and champion of an injured lady, was a gentleman respectful to their legal and natural claims upon their child while maintaining his own: they were to know him and change their tone.

As he was reading the letter upstairs by sentences, his door opened at the answer to a tap. He started; his face was a shield's welcome to the birdlike applicant for admission. Clotilde stood hesitating.

He sent the introducing waiter speeding on his most kellnerish legs, and drew her in.

"Alvan, I have come."

She was like a bird in his hands, palpitating to extinction. He bent over her: "What has happened?"

Trembling, and very pale, hard in her throat she said, "The worst."

"You have spoken to them both subsequent to this?" he shook the letter.

"It is hopeless."

"Both to father and mother?"

"Both. They will not hear your name; they will not hear me speak. I repeat, it is past all hope, all chance of moving them. They hate — hate you, hate me for thinking of you. I had no choice; I wrote at once and followed my letter; I ran through the streets; I pant for want of breath, not want of courage. I prove I have it, Alvan; I have done all I can do."

She was enfolded; she sank on the nest, dropping her eyelids.

But he said nothing. She looked up at him. Her pained pale eyes provoked a closer embrace.

"This would be the home for you if we were flying," said he, glancing round at the room, with a sensation like a shudder. "Tell me what there is to be told."

"Alvan, I have; that is all. They will not listen; they loathe —— Oh! what possesses them!"

"They have not met me yet!"

"They will not, will not ever — no!"

"They must."

"They refuse. Their child, for daring to say she loves you, is detested. Take me — take me away!"

"Run? — facing the enemy?" His countenance was the fiery laugh of a thirster for strife. "They have to be taught the stuff Alvan is made of!"

Clotilde moaned to signify she was sure he nursed an illusion. "I found them celebrating the betrothal of my sister Lotte with the Austrian Count Walburg; I thought it favourable for us. I spoke of you to my mother. Oh, that scene! What she said I cannot recollect: it was a hiss. Then my father. Your name changed his features and his voice. They treated me as impure for mentioning it. You must have deadly enemies. I was unable to recognize either father or mother — they have become transformed. But you see I am here. Courage! you said; and I determined I would show it, and be worthy of you. But I am pursued, I am sure. My father is powerful in this place; we shall barely have time to escape."

Alvan's resolution was taken.

"Some friend — a lady living in the city here — name her, quick! — one you can trust," he said, and fondled her hastily, much as a gentle kind of drillmaster straightens a fair pupil's shoulders. "Yes, you have shown courage. Now it must be submission to me. You shall be no runaway bride, but honoured at the altar. Out of this hotel is the first point. You know some such lady?"

Clotilde tried to remonstrate and to suggest. She could have prophesied certain evil from any evasion of the straight line of flight; she was so sure of it because of her intuition that her courage had done its utmost in casting her on him, and that the remainder within her would be a drawing back. She could not get the word or even the look to encounter his close and warm imperiousness; and, hesitating she noticed where they were together alone. She could not refuse the protection he offered in a person of her own sex; and now, flushing with the thought of where they were together alone, feminine modesty shrivelled at the idea of entreating a man to bear her off, though feminine desperation urged to it. She felt herself very bare of clothing, and she named a lady, a Madame Emerly, living near the hotel. Her heart sank like a stone.

"It is for you!" cried Alvan, keenly sensible of his loss and his generosity in temporarily resigning her for a subsequent triumph. "But my wife shall not be snatched by a thief in the night. Are you not my wife — my golden bride? And you may give me this pledge of it, as if the vows had just been uttered . . . and still I resign you till we speak the vows. It shall not be said of Alvan's wife, in the days of her glory, that she ran to her nuptials through rat-passages."

His pride in his prevailingness thrilled her. She was cooled by her despondency sufficiently to perceive where the centre of it lay, but that centre of self was magnificent; she recovered some of her enthusiasm, thinking him perhaps to be acting rightly; in any case they were united, her step was irrevocable. Her having entered the hotel, her being in this room, certified to that. It seemed to her while she was waiting for the carriage he had ordered that she was already half a wife. She was not conscious of a blush. The sprite in the young woman's mind whispered of fire not burning when one is in the heart of it. And undoubtedly, contemplated from the outside, this room was the heart of fire. An impulse to fall on Alvan's breast and bless him for his chivalrousness had to be kept under lest she should wreck the thing she praised. Otherwise she was not ill at ease. Alvan summoned his gaiety, all his homeliness of tone, to give her composure, and on her quitting the room she was more than ever bound to him, despite her gloomy foreboding.

A maid of her household, a middle-aged woman, gabbling of devotion to her, ran up the steps of the hotel. Her tale was, that the general had roused the city in pursuit of his daughter; and she heard whither Clotilde was going.

Within half an hour, Clotilde was in Madame Emerly's

drawing-room relating her desperate history of love and parental tyranny, assisted by the lover whom she had introduced. Her hostess promised shelter and exhibited sympathy. The whole Teutonic portion of the Continent knew Alvan by reputation. He was insurrectionally notorious in morals and menacingly in politics; but his fine air, handsome face, flowing tongue, and the signal proof of his respect for the lady of his love and deference toward her family, won her personally. She promised the best help she could give them. They were certainly in a romantic situation, such as few women could see and decline their aid to the lovers.

Madame Emerly proved at least her sincerity before many minutes had passed.

Chancing to look out into the street, she saw Clotilde's mother and her betrothed sister stepping up to the house. What was to be done? And was the visit accidental? She announced it, and Clotilde cried out, but Alvan cried louder: "Heaven-directed! and so, let me see her and speak to her — nothing could be better."

Madame Emerly took mute counsel of Clotilde, shaking her own head premonitorily; and then she said: "I think indeed it will be safer, if I am asked, to say you are not here, and I know not where you are."

"Yes! yes!" Clotilde replied: "Oh! do that."

She half turned to Alvan, rigid with an entreaty that hung on his coming voice.

"No!" said Alvan, shocked in both pride and vanity. "Plain-dealing; no subterfuge! Begin with foul falsehood? No. I would not have you burdened, madame, with the shadow of a conventional untruth on our account. And when it would be bad policy? . . . Oh, no, worse than the sin! as the honest cynic says. We will go down to Madame von Rüdiger, and she shall make acquaintance with the man who claims her daughter's hand."

Clotilde rocked in an agony. Her friend was troubled. Both ladies knew what there would be to encounter better than he. But the man, strong in his belief in himself, imposed his will on them.

Alvan and Clotilde clasped hands as they went downstairs to Madame Emerly's reception room. She could hardly speak: "Do not forsake me."

"Is this forsaking?" He could ask it in the deeply questioning tone which supplies the answer.

"Oh, Alvan!" She would have said: "Be warned."

He kissed her fingers. "Trust to me."

She had to wrap her shivering spirit in a blind reliance and utter leaning on him.

She could almost have said: "Know me better;" and she would, sincere as her passion in its shallow vessel was, have been moved to say it for a warning while yet there was time to leave the house instead of turning into that room, had not a remainder of her first exaltation (rapidly degenerating to desperation) inspired her with the thought of her being a part of this handsome, undaunted, triumph-flashing man.

Such a state of blind reliance and utter leaning, however, has a certain tendency to disintegrate the will, and by so doing it prepares the spirit to be a melting prize of the winner.

Men and women alike, who renounce their own individuality by cowering thus abjectly under some other before the storm, are in reality abjuring their idea of that other, and offering themselves up to the genius of Power in whatsoever direction it may chance to be manifested, in whatsoever person. We no sooner shut our eyes than we consent to be prey, we lose the soul of election.

Mark her as she proceeds. For should her hero fail, and she be suffering through his failure and her reliance on him, the blindness of it will seem to her to have been an infinite virtue, anything but her deplorable weakness crouching beneath his show of superhuman strength. And it will seem to her, so long as her sufferings endure, that he deceived her just expectations, and was a vain pretender to the superhuman: — for it was only a superhuman Jew and democrat whom she could have thought of espousing. The pusillanimous are under a necessity to be self-consoled when they are not self-justified: it is their instinctive manner of putting themselves in the right to themselves. The love she bore him, because it was the love his high conceit exacted, hung on success: she was ready to fly with him and love him faithfully: but not without some reason (where reason, we will own, should not quite so coldly obtrude) will it seem to her, that the man who would not fly, and would try the conflict, insisted to stake her love on the issue he provoked. He roused the tempest, he angered the Fates, he tossed her to them; and reason, coldest reason, close as it ever is to the craven's heart in its hour of trial, whispers that he was prompted to fling the gambler's die by the swollen conceit in his fortune rather than by his desire for the prize. That frigid reason of the craven has red-hot perceptions. It spies the spot of truth. Were the spot revealed in the man the whole man, then, so unerring is the eyeshot at him, we should have only to transform ourselves into cowards fronting a crisis to read him through and topple over the Sphinx of life by presenting her the sum of her most mysterious creature in an epigram. But there was as much more in Alvan than any faint-hearted thing, seeing however keenly, could see, as there is more in the world than the epigrams aimed at it contain.

"Courage!" said he: and she tremblingly: "Be careful!" And then they were in the presence of her mother and sister.

Her sister was at the window, hanging her head low, a poor figure. Her mother stood in the middle of the room, and met them full face, with a woman's combative frown of great eyes, in which the stare is a bolt.

"Away with that man! I will not suffer him near me," she cried.

Alvan advanced to her: "Tell me, madame, in God's name, what you have against me."

She swung her back on him. "Go, sir! my husband will know how to deal with one like you. Out of my sight, I say!"

The brutality of this reception of Alvan nerved Clotilde. She went up to him, and laying her hand on his arm, feeling herself almost his equal, said: "Let us go: come. I will not bear to hear you so spoken to. No one shall treat you like that when I am near."

She expected him to give up the hopeless task, after such an experience of the commencement. He did but clasp her hand, assuring the Frau von Rüdiger that no word of hers could irritate him. "Nothing can make me forget that you are Clotilde's mother. You are the mother of the lady I love, and may say what you will to me, madame. I bear it."

"A man spotted with every iniquity the world abhors, and I am to see him holding my daughter by the hand!— it is too abominable! And because there is no one present to chastise him, he dares to address me and talk of his foul passion for my daughter. I repeat: that which you have to do is to go. My ears are shut. You can annoy, you can insult, you cannot move me. Go." She stamped: her aspect spat.

Alvan bowed. Under perfect self-command, he said: "I will go at once to Clotilde's father. I may hope, that with a reasonable man I shall speedily come to an understanding."

She retorted: "Enter his house, and he will have you driven out by his lacqueys."

"Hardly: I am not of those men who are driven from houses," Alvan said, smiling. "But, madame, I will act on your warning, and spare her father, for all sakes, the attempt; seeing he does not yet know whom he deals with. I will write to him."

"Letters from you will be flung back unopened."

"It may, of course, be possible to destroy even my patience, madame."

"Mine, sir, is at an end."

"You reduce us to rely on ourselves; it is the sole alternative."

"You have not waited for that," rejoined Frau von Rüdiger. "You have already destroyed my daughter's reputation by inducing her to leave her father's house and hesitate to return. Oh! you are known. You are known for your dealings with women as well as men. We know you. We have, we pray to God, little more to learn of you. You! ah—thief!"

"Thief!" Alvan's voice rose on hers like the clapping echo of it. She had up the whole angry pride of the man in arms, and could discern that she had struck the wound in his history; but he was terrible to look at, so she made the charge supportable by saying:

"You have stolen my child from me!"

Clotilde raised her throat, shrewish in excitement. "False! He did not. I went to him of my own will, to run from your heartlessness, mother — that I call mother! — and be out of hearing of my father's curses and threats. Yes, to him I fled, feeling that I belonged more to him than to you. And never will I return to you. You have killed my love; I am this man's own because I love him only; him ever! him you abuse, as his partner in life for all it may give! — as his wife! Trample on him, you trample on me. Make black brows at your child for choosing the man, of all men alive, to worship and follow through the world. I do. I am his. I glory in him."

Her gaze on Alvan said: "Now!" Was she not worthy of him now? And would they not go forth together now? Oh! now!

Her gaze was met by nothing like the brilliant counterpart she merited. It was as if she had offered her beauty to a glass, and found a reflection in dull metal. He smiled calmly from her to her mother. He said: "You accuse me of stealing your child, madame. You shall acknowledge that you have wronged me. Clotilde, my Clotilde! may I count on you to do all and everything for me? Is there any sacrifice I could ask that would be too hard for you? Will you at one sign from me go or do as I request you?"

She replied, in an anguish over the chilling riddle of his calmness: "I will," but sprang out of that obedient consent, fearful of over-acting her part of slave to him before her mother, in a ghastly apprehension of the part he was for playing to the same audience. "Yes, I will do all, all that you command. I am yours. I will go with you. Bid me do whatever you can think of, all except bid me go back to the people I have hitherto called mine: — not that!"

"And that is what I have to request of you," said he, with his calm smile brightening and growing more foreign, histrionic, unreadable to her. "And this greatest sacrifice that you can perform for me, are you prepared to do it? Will you?"

She tried to decipher the mask he wore: it was proof against her imploring eyes. "If you can ask me — if you can positively wish it — yes," she said. "But think of what you are doing. Oh! Alvan, not back to them! Think!"

He smiled insufferably. He was bent on winning a parent-blest bride, an unimpeachable wife, a lady handed to him instead of taken, one of the world's polished silver vessels.

"Think that you are doing this for me!" said he. "It is for my sake. And now, madame, I give you back your daughter. You see she is mine to give, she obeys me, and I — though it can be only for a short time — give her back to you. She goes with you purely because it is my wish: do not forget that. And so, madame, I have the honour," he bowed profoundly.

He turned to Clotilde and drew her within his arm. "What you have done in obedience to my wish, my beloved, shall never be forgotten. Never can I sufficiently thank you. I know how much it has cost you. But here is the end of your trials. All the rest is now my task. Rely on me with your whole heart. Let them not misuse you: otherwise do their bidding. Be sure of my knowing how you are treated, and at the slightest act of injustice I shall be beside you to take you to myself. Be sure of that, and be not unhappy. They shall not keep you from me for long. Submit a short while to the will of your parents: mine you will find the stronger. Resolve it in your soul that I, your lover, cannot fail, for it is impossible to me to waver. Consider me as the one fixed light in your world, and look to me. Soon, then! Have patience, be true, and we are one!"

He kissed cold lips, he squeezed an inanimate hand. The horribly empty sublimity of his behaviour appeared to her in her mother's contemptuous face.

His eyes were on her as he released her and she stood alone. She seemed a dead thing; but the sense of his having done gloriously in mastering himself to give these worldly people of hers a lesson and proof that he could within due measure bow to their laws and customs, dispelled the brief vision of her unfitness to be left. The compressed energy of the man under his conscious display of a great-minded deference to the claims of family ties and duties, intoxicated him. He thought but of the present achievement and its just effect: he had cancelled a bad reputation among these people, from whom he was about to lead forth a daughter for Alvan's wife, and he reasoned by the grandeur of his exhibition of generosity — which was brought out in strong relief when he delivered his retiring bow to the Frau von Rüdiger's shoulder — that the worst was over; he had to deal no more with silly women: now for Clotilde's father! Women were privileged to oppose their senselessness to the divine fire: men could not retreat behind such defences; they must meet him on the common ground of men, where this constant battler had never yet encountered a reverse.

Clotilde's cold staring gaze, a little livelier to wonderment than to reflection, observed him to be scrupulous of the formalities in the diverse character of his parting salutations to her mother, her sister, and the lady of the house. He was going — he could actually go and leave her! She stretched herself to him faintly; she let it be seen that she did so as much as she had force to make it visible. She saw him smiling incomprehensibly, like a winner of the field to be left to the enemy. She could get nothing from him but that insensible round smile, and she took the ebbing of her poor effort for his rebuff.

"You that offered yourself in flight to him who once proposed it, he had the choice of you and he abjured you. He has cast you off!"

She phrased it in speech to herself. It was incredible, but it was clear: he had gone.

The room was vacant; the room was black and silent as a dungeon.

"He will not have you: he has handed you back to them the more readily to renounce you."

She framed the words half aloud in a moan as she glanced at her mother heaving in stern triumph, her sister drooping, Madame Emerly standing at the window.

The craven's first instinct for safety, quick as the cavern lynx for light, set her on the idea that she was abandoned: it whispered of quietness if she submitted.

And thus she reasoned: Had Alvan taken her, she would not have been guilty of more than a common piece of love-desperation in running to him, the which may be love's glory when marriage crowns it. By his rejecting her and leaving her, he rendered her not only a runaway, but a castaway. It was not natural that he should leave her; not natural in him to act his recent part; but he had done it; consequently she was at the mercy of those who might pick her up. She was, in her humiliation and dread, all of the moment, she could see to no distance; and judging of him, feeling for herself, within that contracted circle of sensation — sure, from her knowledge of her cowardice, that he had done unwisely — she became swayed about like a castaway in soul, until her distinguishing of his mad recklessness in the challenge of a power greater than his own grew present with her as his personal cruelty to the woman who had flung off everything, flung herself on the tempestuous deeps, on his behalf. And here she was, left to float or founder! Alvan had gone. The man rageing over the room, abusing her "infamous lover, the dirty Jew, the notorious thief, scoundrel, gallowsbird," etc., etc., frightful epithets, not to be transcribed — was her father. He had come, she knew not how. Alvan had tossed her to him.

Abuse of a lover is ordinarily retorted on in the lady's heart by the brighter perception of his merits; but when the heart is weak, the creature suffering shame, her lover the cause of it, and seeming cruel, she is likely to lose all perception and bend like a flower pelted. Her cry to him : "If you had been wiser, this would not have been!" will sink to the inward meditation: "If he had been truer!" — and though she does not necessarily think him untrue for charging him with it, there is already a loosening of the bonds where the accusation has begun. They are not broken because they are loosened: still the loosening of them makes it possible to cut them with less of a snap and less pain.

Alvan had relinquished her he loved to brave the tempest in a frail small boat, and he certainly could not have apprehended the furious outbreak she was exposed to. She might so far have exonerated him had she been able to reflect; but she whom he had forced to depend on him in blind reliance, now opened her eyes on an opposite power exercising material rigours. After having enjoyed extraordinary independence for a young woman, she was treated as a refractory child, literally marched through the streets in the custody of her father, who clutched her by the hair — Alvan's beloved golden locks! — and held her under terror of a huge forester's weapon, that he had seized at the first tidings of his daughter's flight to the Jew. He seemed to have a grim indifference to exposure; contempt, with a sense of the humour of it: and this was a satisfaction to him, founded on his practical observance of two or three maxims quite equal to the fullest knowledge of women for rightly managing them: preferable, inasmuch as they are simpler, and, by merely cracking a whip, bring her back to the post, instead of wasting time by hunting her as she likes to run. Police were round his house. The General chattered and shouted of the desperate lawlessness and larcenies of that Jew — the things that Jew would attempt. He dragged her indoors, muttering of his policy in treating her at last to a wholesome despotism. This was the medicine for her — he knew her! Whether he did or not, he knew the potency of his physic. He knew that osiers can be made to bend. With a frightful noise of hammering, he himself nailed up the window-shutters of the room she was locked in hard and fast, and he left her there and roared across the household that any one holding communication with the prisoner should be shot like a dog. This was a manifestation of power in a form more convincing than the orator's.

She was friendless, abused, degraded, benighted in broad daylight; abandoned by her lover. She sank on the floor of the room, conceiving with much strangeness of sentiment under these hard stripes of misfortune, that reality had come. The monster had hold of her. She was isolated, fed like a dungeoned captive. She had nothing but our natural obstinacy to hug, or seem to do so when wearifulness reduced her to cling to the semblance of it only. "I marry Alvan!" was her iterated answer to her father, on his visits to see whether he had yet broken her; and she spoke with the desperate firmness of weak creatures that strive to nail themselves to the sound of it. He listened and named his time for returning. The tug between rigour and endurance continued for about forty hours. She then thought, in an exhaustion: "Strange that my father should be so fiercely excited against this man! Can he have reasons I have not heard of?" Her father's unwonted harshness suggested the question in her quailing nature, which was beginning to have a movement to kiss the whip. The question set her thinking of the reasons she knew. She saw them involuntarily from the side of parents, and they wore a sinister appearance; in reality her present scourging was due to them as well as to Alvan's fatal decision. Her misery was traceable to his conduct and his judgement — both bad. And yet all this while he might be working to release her, near upon rescuing! She swung round to the side of her lover against these executioner parents, and scribbled to him as well as she could under the cracks in her window-shutters, urging him to appear. She spent her heart on it. A note to her friend, the English lady, protested her love for Alvan, but with less abandonment, with a frozen resignation to the loss of him — all around her was so dark! By-and-by there was a scratching at her door. The maid whom she trusted brought her news of Alvan: outside the door and in, the maid and mistress knelt. Hope flickered up in the bosom of Clotilde: the whispers were exchanged through the partition.

"Where is he?"
"Gone."
"But where?"
"He has left the city."

Clotilde pushed the letter for her friend under the door: that one for Alvan she retained, stung by his desertion of her, and thinking practically that it was useless to aim a letter at a man without an address. She did not ask herself whether the maid's information was honest, for she wanted to despair, as the exhausted want to lie down.

She wept through the night. It was one of those nights of the torrents of tears which wash away all save the adamantine within us, if there be ought of that besides the breathing structure. The reason why she wept with so delirious a persistency was, that her nature felt the necessity for draining her of her self-pitifulness, knowing that it nourished the love whereby she was tormented. They do not weep thus who have a heart for the struggle. In the morning she was a dried channel of tears, no longer self-pitiful; careless of herself, as she thought: in other words, unable any further to contend. Reality was too strong! This morning her sisters came to her room imploring her to yield: — if she married Alvan, what could be their prospects as the sisters-in-law of such a man? — her betrothed sister Lotte could not hope to espouse Count Walburg: — Alvan's name was infamous in society; their house would be a lazar-house, they would be condemned to seclusion. A favourite brother followed, with sympathy that set her tears running again, and arguments she could not answer: — how could he hold up his head in his regiment as the relative of the scandalous Jew democrat? He would have to leave the service, or be duelling with his brother officers every other day of his life, for rightly or wrongly Alvan was abhorred, and his connection would be fatal to them all, perhaps to her father's military and diplomatic career principally: the head of their house would be ruined. She was compelled to weep again by having no other reply. The tears were now mixed drops of pity for her absent lover and her family; she was already disunited from him when she shed them, feeling that she was dry rock to herself, heartless as many bosoms drained of self-pity will become.

Incapable of that any further, she leaned still in that direction and had a languid willingness to gain outward comfort. To be caressed a little by her own kindred before she ceased to live was desirable after her heavy scourging. She wished for the touches of affection, knowing them to be selfish, but her love of life and hard view of its reality made them seem a soft reminder of what life had been. Alvan had gone. Her natural blankness of imagination read his absence as an entire relinquishment; it knelled in a vacant chamber. He had gone; he had committed an irretrievable error, he had given up a fight of his own vain provoking, that was too severe for him: he was not the lover he fancied himself, or not the lord of men she had fancied him. Her excessive misery would not suffer a picture of him, not one clear recollection of him, to stand before her. He who should have been at hand, had gone, and she was fearfully beset, almost lifeless; and being abandoned, her blank night of imagination felt that there was nothing left for her save to fall upon those nearest.

She gave her submission to her mother. In her mind, during the last wrestling with a weakness that was alternately her love and her cowardice, the interpretation of the act ran: "He may come, and I am his *if* he comes: and if not, I am bound to my people." He had taught her to rely on him blindly, and thus she did it inanimately while cutting herself loose from him. In a similar mood, the spiritual waverer vows to believe if the saint will appear. However, she submitted. Then there was joy in the family, and she tasted their caresses.

## CHAPTER IX.

AFTER his deed of loftiness Alvan walked to his hotel, where the sight of the room Clotilde had entered that morning caught his breath. He proceeded to write his first letter to General von Rüdiger, repressing his heart's intimations that he had stepped out of the friendly path, and was on a strange and tangled one. The sense of power in him was leonine enough to promise the forcing of a way whithersoever the path: yet did that ghost of her figure across the room haunt him with searching eyes. They set him spying over himself at an actor who had not needed to be acting his part, brilliant though it was. He crammed his energy into his idea of the part, to carry it forward victoriously. Before the world, it would without question redound to his credit, and he heard the world acclaiming him: —

"Alvan's wife was honourably won, as became the wife of a Doctor of Law, from the bosom of her family, when he could have had her in the old lawless fashion, for a call to a coachman! Alvan, the republican, is eminently a citizen. Consider his past life by that test of his character."

He who had many times defied the world in hot rebellion, had become, through his desire to cherish a respectable passion, if not exactly slavish to it, subservient, as we see royal personages, that are happy to be on bowing terms with the multitude bowing lower. Lower, of course, the multitude must bow, to inspire an august serenity; but the nod they have in exchange for it is not an independent one. Ceasing to be a social rebel, he conceived himself as a recognized dignitary, and he passed under the bondage of that position.

Clotilde had been in this room; she had furnished proof that she could be trusted now. She had committed herself, perished as a maiden of society, and her parents, even the senseless mother, must see it and decide by it. The General would bring her to reason: General von Rüdiger was a man of the world. An honourable son-in-law could not but be acceptable to him — now, at least. And such a son-in-law would ultimately be the pride of his house. "A flower from thy garden, friend, and my wearing it shall in good time be cause for some parental gratification."

The letter despatched, Alvan paced his chamber with the ghost of Clotilde. He was presently summoned to meet Count Walburg and another intimate of the family, in the hotel downstairs. These gentlemen brought no message from General von Rüdiger: their words were directed to extract a promise from him that he would quit his pursuit of Clotilde, and of course he refused; they hinted that the General might have official influence to get him expelled the city, and he referred them to the proof; but he looked beyond the words at a new something of extraordinary and sinister aspect revealed to him in their manner of treating his pretensions to the hand of the lady.

He had not yet perfectly seen the view the world took of him, because of his armed opposition to the world; nor could he rightly reflect on it yet, being too anxious to sign the peace. He felt as it were a blow startling him from sleep. His visitors tasked themselves to be strictly polite; they did not undervalue his resources for commanding respect between man and man. The strange matter was behind their bearing, which indicated the positive impossibility of the union of Clotilde with one such as he, and struck at the curtain covering his history. He could not raise it to thunder his defence of himself, or even allude to the implied contempt of his character: with a boiling gorge he was obliged to swallow both the history and the insult, returning them the equivalent of their courtesies, though it was on his lips to thunder heavily.

A second endeavour, in an urgent letter before nightfall to gain him admission to head-quarters, met the same repulse as the foregoing. The bearer of it was dismissed without an answer.

Alvan passed a night of dire disturbance. The fate of the noble Genoese conspirator, slipping into still harbour water on the step from boat to boat, and borne down by the weight of his armour in the moment of the ripeness of his plot at midnight, when the signal for action sparkled to lighten across the ships and forts, had touched him in his boy's readings, and he found a resemblance of himself to Fiesco, stopped as he was by a base impediment, tripped ignominiously, choked by the weight of the powers fitting him for battle. A man such as Alvan, arrested on his career by an opposition to his enrolment of a bride! — think of it! What was this girl in a life like his? But, oh! the question was no sooner asked than the thought that this girl had been in this room illuminated the room, telling him she might have been his own this instant, confounding him with an accusation of madness for rejecting her. Why had he done it? Surely women, weak women, must be at times divinely inspired. She warned him against the step. But he, proud of his armoury, went his way. He choked, he suffered the torture of the mailed Genoese going under; worse, for the drowner's delirium swirls but a minute in the gaping brain, while he had to lie all night at the mercy of the night.

He was only calmer when morning came. Night has little mercy for the self-reproachful, and for a strong man denouncing the folly of his error, it has none. The bequest of the night was a fever of passion; and upon that fever the light of morning cleared his head to weigh the force opposing him. He gnawed the paradox, that it was huge because it was petty, getting a miserable sour sustenance out of his consciousness of the position it explained. Great enemies, great undertakings, would have revived him as they had always revived and fortified. But here was a stolid small obstacle, scarce assailable on its own level; and he had chosen that it should be attacked through its own laws and forms. By shutting a door, by withholding an answer to his knocks, the thing reduced him to hesitation. And the thing had weapons to shoot at him; his history, his very blood, stood open to its shafts; and the sole quality of a giant which he could show to front it, was the breadth of one for a mark.

These direct perceptions of the circumstances were played on by the fever he drew from his Fiesco bed. Accuracy of vision in our crises is not so uncommon as the proportionate equality of feeling: we do indeed frequently see with eyes of just measurement while we are conducting ourselves like madmen. The facts are seen, and yet the spinning nerves will change their complexion; and without enlarging or minimizing, they will alternate their effect on us immensely through the colour presenting them — now sombre, now hopeful: doing its work of extravagance upon perceptibly plain matter. The fitful colour is the fever. He must win her, for he never yet had failed — he had lost her by his folly! She was his — she was torn from him! She would come at his bidding — she would cower to her tyrants! The thought of her was life and death in his frame, bright heaven and the abyss. At one beat of the heart she swam to his arms, at another he was straining over darkness. And whose the fault?

He rose out of his amazement crying it with a roar, and foreignly beholding himself. He pelted himself with epithets; his worst enemies could not have been handier in using them. From Alvan to Alvan, they signified such an earthquake in a land of splendid structures as shatters to dust the pride of the works of men. He was down among them, lower than the herd, rolling in vulgar epithets that, attached to one like him, became of monstrous distortion. O fool! dolt! blind ass! tottering idiot! drunken masquerader! miserable Jack Knave, performing suicide with that blessed coxcomb air of curling a lock! — Clotilde! Clotilde! Where has one read a story of a man who had the jewel of jewels in his hand, and flung it into the deeps, thinking that he flung a pebble? Fish, fool, fish! and fish till Doomsday! There's nothing but your fool's face in the water to be got to bite at the bait you throw, fool! Fish for the flung-away beauty, and hook your shadow of a Bottom's head! What impious villain was it refused the gift of the gods, that he might have it bestowed on him according to his own prescription of the ceremonies! They laugh! By Orcus! how they laugh! The laughter of the gods is the lightning of death's irony over mortals. Can they have a finer subject than a giant gone fool?

Tears burst from him: tears of rage, regret, self-lashing. O for yesterday! He called aloud for the recovery of yesterday, bellowed, groaned. A giant at war with pygmies, having nought but their weapons, having to fight them on his knees, to fight them with the right hand while smiting himself with the left, has too much upon him to keep his private dignity in order. He was the same in his letters — a Cyclops hurling rocks and raising the seas to shipwreck. Dignity was cast off; he came out naked. Letters to Clotilde, and to the baroness, to the friend nearest him just then, Colonel von Tresten, calling them to him, were dashed to paper in this naked frenzy, and he could rave with all the truth of life, that to have acted the idiot, more than the loss of the woman, was the ground of his anguish. Each antecedent of his career had been a step of strength, and success departed. The woman was but a fragment of the tremendous wreck; the woman was utterly diminutive, yet she was the key of the reconstruction; the woman won, he would be himself once more: and feeling that, his passion for her swelled to full tide and she became a towering splendour whereat his eyeballs ached, she became a melting armful that shook him to big bursts of tears.

The feeling of the return of strength was his love in force. The giant in him loved her warmly. Her sweetness, her archness, the opening of her lips, their way of holding closed, and her brightness of wit, her tender eyelashes, her appreciating looks, her sighing, the thousand varying shades of her motions and her features interflowing like a lighted water, swam to him one by one like so many handmaiden messengers distinctly beheld of the radiant indistinct whom he adored with more of spirit in his passion than before this tempest. A giant going through a giant's contortions, fleshly as the race of giants, and gross, coarse, dreadful, likely to be horrible when whipped and stirred to the dregs, Alvan was great-hearted: he could love in his giant's fashion, love and lay down life for the woman he loved, though the nature of the passion was not heavenly; or for the friend — who would have to excuse him often; or for the public cause — which was to minister to his appetites. He was true man, a native of earth, and if he could not quit his huge personality to pipe spiritual music during a storm of trouble, being a soul wedged in the gnarled wood of the standing giant oak, and giving mighty sound of timber at strife rather than the angelical cry, he suffered, as he loved, to his depths.

We have not to plumb the depths; he was not heroic, but hugely man. Love and man sometimes meet for noble concord; the strings of the hungry instrument are not all so rough that Love's touch on them is indistinguishable from the rattling of the wheels within; certain herald harmonies have been heard. But Love, which purifies and enlarges us, and sets free the soul, Love visiting a fleshly frame must have time and space, and some help of circumstance, to give the world assurance that the man is a temple fit for the rites. Out of romances, he is not melodiously composed. And in a giant are various giants to be slain, or thoroughly subdued, ere this divinity is taken for leader. It is not done by miracle.

As it happened cruelly for Alvan, the woman who had become the radiant indistinct in his desiring mind was one whom he knew to be of a shivery steadfastness. His plucking her from another was neither wonderful nor indefensible; they two were suited as no other two could be; the handsome boy who had gone through a form of plighting with her was her slave, and she required for her mate a master: she felt it and she sided to him quite naturally, moved by the sacred direction of the acknowledgment of a mutual fitness. Twice, however, she had relapsed on the occasions of his absence, and owning his power over her when they were together again, she sowed the fatal conviction that he held her at present, and that she was a woman only to be held at present, by the palpable grasp of his physical influence. Partly it was correct, not entirely, seeing that she kept the impression of a belief in him even when she drifted away through sheer weakness, but it was the single positive view he had of her, and it was fatal, for it begat a devil of impatience.

"They are undermining her now — now — now!"

He started himself into busy frenzies to reach to her, already indifferent to the means, and waxing increasingly reckless as he fed on his agitation. Some faith in her, even the little she deserved, would have arrested him: unhappily he had less than she, who had enough to nurse the dim sense of his fixity, and sank from him only in her heart's faintness, but he, when no longer flattered by the evidence of his mastery, took her for sand. Why, then, had he let her out of his grasp? The horrid echoed interrogation flashed a hideous view of the woman. But how had he come to be guilty of it? he asked himself again; and, without answering him, his counsellors to that poor wisdom set to work to complete it: Giant Vanity urged Giant Energy to make use of Giant Duplicity. He wrote to Clotilde, with one voice quoting the law in their favour, with another commanding her to break it. He gathered and drilled a legion of spies, and showered his gold in bribes and plots to get the letter to her, to get an interview — one human word between them.

## CHAPTER X.

His friend Colonel von Tresten was beside him when he received the enemy's counter-stroke. Count Walburg and his companion brought a letter from Clotilde — no reply; a letter renouncing him.

Briefly, in cold words befitting the act, she stated that the past must be dead between them; for the future she belonged to her parents; she had left the city. She knew not where he might be, her letter concluded, but henceforward he should know that they were strangers.

Alvan held out the deadly paper when he had read the contents; he smote a forefinger on it and crumpled it in his hand. That was the dumb oration of a man shocked by the outrage upon passionate feeling to the state of brute.

His fist, outstretched to the length of his arm, shook the reptile letter under a terrible frown.

Tresten saw that he supposed himself to be perfectly master of his acts because he had not spoken, and had managed to preserve the ordinary courtesies.

"You have done your commission," the colonel said to Count Walburg, whose companion was not disposed to go without obtaining satisfactory assurances, and pressed for them.

Alvan fastened on him. "You adopt the responsibility of this?" He displayed the letter.

"I do."

"It lies."

Tresten remarked to Count Walburg: "These visits are provocations."

"They are not so intended," said the count, bowing pacifically. His friend was not a man of the sword, and was not under the obligation to accept an insult. They left the letter to do its work.

Big natures in their fits of explosiveness must be taken by flying shots, as dwarfs peep on a monster, or the Scythian attacked a phalanx. Were we to hear all the roarings of the shirted Heracles, a world of comfortable little ones would doubt the unselfishness of his love of Dejaneira. Yes, really; they would think it was not a chivalrous love: they would consider that he thought of himself too much. They would doubt, too, of his being a gentleman! Partial glimpses of him, one may fear, will be discomposing to simple natures. There was a short black eruption. Alvan controlled it, to ask hastily what the baroness thought and what she had heard of Clotilde. Tresten made sign that it was nothing of the best.

"See! my girl has hundreds of enemies, and I, only I, know her and can defend her — weak, base, shallow trickster, traitress that she is!" cried Alvan, and came down in a thundershower upon her: "Yesterday — the day before — when? just now, here, in this room; gave herself — and now!" He bent, and immediately straightening his back, addressed Colonel von Tresten as her calumniator, "Say your worst of her, and I say I will make of that girl the peerless woman of earth! I! in earnest! it's no dream.

She can be made. . . . O God! the beast has turned tail! I knew she could. There's three of beast to one of goddess in her, and set her alone, and let her be hunted and I not by, beast it is with her! cowardly skulking beast — the noblest and very bravest under my wing! Incomprehensible to you, Tresten? But who understands women! You hate her. Do not. She's a riddle, but no worse than the rest of the tangle. She gives me up? Pooh! She writes it. She writes anything. And that vilest, I say, I will make more enviable, more — Clotilde!" he thundered her signature in an amazement, broken suddenly by the sight of her putting her name to the letter. She had done that, *written her name* to the renunciation of him! No individual could bear the sight of such a crime, and no suffering man could be appeased by a single victim to atone for it. Her sex must be slaughtered; he raged against the woman; she became that ancient poisonous thing, *the woman;* his fury would not distinguish her as Clotilde, though the name had started him, and it was his knowledge of the particular sinner which drew down his curses on the sex. He twisted his body, hugging at his breast as if he had her letter sticking in his ribs. The letter was up against his ribs, and he thumped it, crushed it, patted it; he kissed it, and flung it, stamped on it, and was foul-mouthed. Seeing it at his feet, he bent to it like a man snapped in two, lamenting, bewailing himself, recovering sight of her fragmentarily. It stuck in his ribs, and in scorn of the writer, and sceptical of her penning it, he tugged to pull it out, and broke the shaft, but left the rankling arrow-head: — she had traced the lines, and though tyranny racked her to do that thing, his agony followed her hand over the paper to her name, which fixed and bit in him like the deadly-toothed arrow-head called asp, and there was no uprooting it. The thing lived; her deed was the woman; there was no separating them: witness it in love murdered.

O that woman! She has murdered love. She has blotted love completely out. She is the arch-thief and assassin of mankind — the female Apollyon. He lost sight of her in the prodigious iniquity covering her sex with a cowl of night, and it was what women are, what women will do, the one and all alike simpering simulacra that men find them to be, soulless, clogs on us, blood-suckers! until a feature of the particular sinner peeped out on him, and brought the fresh agony of a reminder of his great-heartedness. "For that woman — Tresten, you know me — I would have sacrificed for that woman fortune and life, my hope, my duty, my immortality. She knew it, and she — look!" he unwrinkled the letter carefully for it to be legible, and clenched it in a ball — " Signs her name, signs her name, her name! — God of heaven! it would be incredible in a holy chronicle — signs her name to the infamous harlotry! See: 'Clotilde von Rüdiger.' It's her writing; that's her signature: 'Clotilde' in full. You'd hardly fancy that, now? But look!" the colonel's eyelids were blinking, and Alvan dinted his finger-nail under her name: "there it is: *Clotilde:* signed shamelessly. Just as she might have written to one of her friends about bonnets, and balls, and books! — Henceforward *strangers*, she and I?"

His laughter, even to Tresten, a man of camps, sounded profane as a yell beneath a cathedral dome. "Why, the woman has been in my hands — I released her, spared her, drilled brain and blood, ransacked all the code, to do her homage and honour in every mortal way; and we two strangers! Do you hear that, Tresten? Why, if you had seen her! — she was lost, and I, this man she now pierces with ice, kept hell down under bolt and bar — worse, I believe, broke a good woman's heart! — that never a breath should rise that could accuse her on suspicion, or in malice, or by accident, justly, or with a shadow of truth. '*I think it best for us both.*' So she thinks for me! She not only decides, she thinks; she is the active principle; 't is mine to submit. — A certain presumption was in that girl always. Ha! do you hear me? Her letter may sting, it shall not dupe. Strangers? Poor fool! You see plainly she was nailed down to write the thing. This letter is a flat lie. She can lie — Oh! born to the art! born to it! — lies like a Saint tricking Satan! But she says she has left the city. Now to find her!"

He began marching about the room with great strides. "I'll have the whole Continent up; her keepers shall have no rest; I'll have them by the Law Courts, and by stratagem, and, if law and cunning fail, force. I have sworn it. I have done all that honour can ask of a man; more than any man, to my knowledge, would have done, and now it's war. I declare war on them. They will have it! I mean to take that girl from them — snatch or catch! The girl is my girl, and if there are laws against my having my own, to powder with the laws! Well, and do you suppose me likely to be beaten? Then Cicero was a fiction, and Cæsar a people's legend. Not if they are history, and eloquence and commandership have power over the blood and souls of men. First, I write to her!"

His friend suggested that he knew not where she was. But already the pen was at work, the brain pouring as from a pitcher.

Writing was blood-letting, and the interminable pages drained him of his fever. As he wrote, she grew more radiant, more indistinct, more fiercely desired. The concentration of his active mind directed his whole being on the track of Clotilde, idealizing her beyond human. That last day when he had seen her appeared to him as the day of days. That day was Clotilde herself, she in person; he saw it as the woman, and saw himself translucent in the great luminousness; and behind it all was dark, as in front. That one day was the sun of his life. It had been a day of rain, and he beheld it in memory just as it had been, with the dark threaded air, the dripping streets; and he glorified it past all daily radiance. His letter was a burning hymn to the day. His moral grandeur on the day made him live as part of the splendour. Was it possible for the woman who had seen him then to be faithless to him? The swift deduction from his own feelings cleansed her of a suspicion to the contrary, and he became light-hearted. He hummed an air when he had finished his letter to her.

Councils with his adherents and couriers were held, and some were despatched to watch the house and slip the letter to her maid; others were told off to bribe and hound their way on the track of Clotilde. His gold rained into their hands with the directions.

Colonel von Tresten was the friend of his attachment to the baroness: a friend of both, and a warm one. Men coming into contact with Alvan took their shape of friend or enemy sharply, for he was friend or enemy of no dubious feature, devoted to them he loved, and a battery on them he opposed. The colonel had been the confidant of the baroness's grief over this love-passion of Alvan's, and her resignation. He shared her doubts of Clotilde's nobility. of character: the reports were not favourable to the young lady. But the baroness and he were of one opinion, that Alvan in love was not likely to be governable by prudent counsel. He dropped a word of the whispers of Clotilde's volatility.

Alvan nodded his perfect assent. "She is that, she is anything you like; you cannot exaggerate her for good or evil. She is matchless, colour her as you please." Adopting the tone of argument, he said: "She writes that letter. Well? It is her writing, and the moment I am sure of it as hers, I would not have it unwritten. I love it!" He looked maddish with his love of the horrible thing, and resumed soberly: "The point is, that she has the charm for *me*. She is plastic in my hands. Other men would waste the treasure. I make of her what I will, and she knows it, and knows that she hangs on me to flourish worthily. I breathe the very soul of the woman into her. As for that letter of hers —" it burnt him this time to speak of the letter: "she may write and write! She's weak, thin, a reed; she — let her be! Say of her when she plays beast — she is absent from Alvan! I can forgive. The letter's nothing; it means nothing — except 'Thou fool, Alvan, to let me go.' Yes, that! Her people are acting tyrant with her — as legally they have no right to do in this country, and I shall prove it to them. When I have gained admission to her — and I soon shall: it can't be refused: I am off to the head of her father's office to-morrow, and I have only to represent the state of affairs to the Minister *in my language* to obtain his authority to demand admission to her: — then, friend, you will see! I lift my finger, and you will see! At my request she went back to her mother. I have but to beckon."

He had cooled to the happy assurance of his authority over her, all the giants of his system being well in action, and when that is the case with a big nature it is at rest, or such is the condition of repose granted it in life.

On the morrow he was off to batter at doors which would have expected rather the summons of an armed mob at his heels than the strange cry of the Radical man maltreated by love.

## CHAPTER XI.

THE story of Clotilde's departure from the city, like that of Alvan's, communicated to her by her maid, was an anticipation of the truth, disseminated by her parents. She was removed when the swarm of spies and secret letter-bearers were attaining a position of dignity through the rumour of legal gentlemen about to direct the movements of the besieging army.

A stir seemed to her to prognosticate a rescue and she went not unwillingly. To be in motion, to see roadside faces, pricked her senses with some hope. She had gained the peace she needed, and in that state her heart began to be agitated by a fresh awakening, luxurious at first rather than troublesome. She had sunk so low that the light of Alvan seemed too distant for a positive expectation of him; but few approached her whom she did not fancy under strange disguises: the gentlemen were servants, the blouses were gentlemen; she looked wistfully at old women bearing baskets, for the forbidden fruit to peep out in the form of an envelope. All passed her blankly, noticing her eyes.

The journey was short; she was taken to a place a little beyond the head of the lake, and there, though she had liberty to breathe the air, fast fixed within the walls of a daily sameness that became gradually the hum of voices accusing Alvan of one in excess of the many sins laid against him by his enemies. Was he not possibly an empty pretender to power — a mere great talker? Her bit of liberty increased her chafing at the deadly monotony of this existence, and envenomed the accusation by seeming to push her forth quite half way to meet him, if he would but come or show sign! She impetuously vindicated him from the charge of crediting the sincerity of any words she might have committed to paper at the despotic dictation of her father. Oh, no; Alvan could not be guilty of such folly as that; he could not; it would be to suppose him unacquainted with her, ignorant of the nature of women. He would know that she wrote the words — why? She could not perfectly recollect how she had come to write them, and found it easier to extinguish the act of having written them at all, which was done by the angry recurrence to his failure to intervene now when the drama cried for his godlike appearance. Perhaps he was really unacquainted with her — thought her stronger than she was! The idea reflected a shadow on his intelligence. She was not in a situation that could bear of her blaming herself.

While she was thus devoured by the legions of her enfeebled wits, Clotilde was assiduously courted by her family, and her father from time to time brought pen and paper for her to write anew from his dictation. He was pleased to hail her as his fair secretary, and when the letters were unimportant she wrote flowingly, happy to be praised. They were occasionally addressed to friends; she discovered herself writing one to the professor, in which he was about to be informed that she had resolved to banish Alvan from her mind for ever. She stopped; her heart stopped; the pen fell from her hand, in loathing. Her father warily bade her proceed. She could not; she signified it choking. Only a few days before she had written to the professor exultingly of her engagement. She refused to belie herself in such a manner; retrospectively her rapid contradictions appeared impossible; the picture of her was not human, and she gave out a negative of her whole frame convulsed, whereat the General was not slow to remind her of the scourgings she had undergone by a sudden burst of his wrath. He knew the proper physic. "You girls want the lesson we read to skittish recruits; you shall have it. Write: '*He is now as nothing to me.*' You shall write that you hate him, if you hesitate! Why, you unreasonable slut, you have given him up; you have told him you have given him up, and what objection can you have to telling others now you have done it?"

"I was forced to it, body and soul!" cried Clotilde,

sobbing and bursting into desperation out of a weak show of petulance that she had put on to propitiate him. "If I have to tell, I will tell how it was. For that my heart is unchanged, and Alvan is, and will be, my lord, all the world may see. I would rather write that I hate him."

"You write, *the man is now as nothing to me!*" said her father, dashing his finger in a fiery zig-zag along the line for her pen to follow. "Or else, my girl, you've been playing us a pretty farce!" He strung himself for a mad gallop of wrath, gave her a shudder, and relapsed. "No, no, you're wiser, you're a better girl than that. Write it. I must have it written — here, come! The worst is over; the rest is child's play. Come, take the pen, I'll guide your hand."

The pen was fixed in her hand, and the first words formed. They looked such sprawling skeletons that Clotilde had the comfort of feeling sure they would be discerned as the work of compulsion. So she wrote on mechanically, solacing herself for what she did with vows of future revolt. Alvan had a saying, that *want of courage is want of sense;* and she remembered his illustration of how sense would nourish courage by scattering the fear of death, if we would only grasp the thought that we sink to oblivion gladly at night, and, most of us, quit it reluctantly in the morning. She shut her eyes while writing; she fancied death would be welcome; and as she certainly had sense, she took it for the promise of courage. She flattered herself by believing, therefore, that she who did not object to die was only awaiting the cruelly-delayed advent of her lover to be almost as brave as he — the feminine of him. With these ideas in her head much clearer than when she wrote the couple of lines to Alvan — for then her head was reeling, she was then beaten and prostrate — she signed her name to a second renunciation of him, and was aware of a flush of self-reproach at the simple suspicion of *his* being deceived by it; it was an insult to his understanding. Full surely the professor would not be deceived, and a lover with a heart to reach to her and read her could never be hoodwinked by so palpable a piece of slavishness. She was indeed slavish; the apology necessitated the confession. But that promise of courage, coming of her ownership of sense, vindicated her prospectively; she had so little of it that she embraced it as a present possession, and she made it Alvan's task to put it to the trial. Hence it became Alvan's offence if, owing to his absence, she could be charged with behaving badly. Her generosity pardoned him his inexplicable delay to appear in his might: "But see what your continued delay *causes!*" she said, and her tone was merely sorrowful.

She had forgotten her signature to the letter to the professor when his answer arrived. The sight of the handwriting of one of her lover's faithfullest friends was like a peal of bells to her, and she tore the letter open, and began to blink and spell at a strange language, taking the frosty sentences piecemeal. He begged her to be firm in her resolution, give up Alvan and obey her parents! This man of high intelligence and cultivation wrote like a provincial schoolmistress moralizing. Though he knew the depth of her passion for Alvan, and had within the month received her lark-song of her betrothal, he, this man — if living man he could be thought — counselled her to endeavour to deserve the love and respect of her parents, alluded to Alvan's age and her better birth, approved her resolve to consult the wishes of her family, and in fine was as rank a traitor to friendship as any chronicled. Out on him! She swept him from earth.

And she had built some of her hopes on the professor.

"False friend!" she cried.

She wept over Alvan for having had so false a friend.

There remained no one that could be expected to intervene with a strong arm save the baroness. The professor's emphasized approval of her resolve to consult the wishes of her family was a shocking hypocrisy, and Clotilde thought of the contrast to it in her letter to the baroness. The tripping and stumbling, prettily awkward little tone of gosling innocent new from its egg, throughout the letter, was a triumph of candour. She repeated passages, paragraphs, of the letter, assuring herself that such affectionately reverential prattle would have moved *her*, and with the strongest desire to cast her arms about the writer: it had been composed to be moving to a woman, to any woman. The old woman was entreated to bestow her blessing on the young one, all in Arcadia, and let the young one nestle to the bosom she had not an idea of robbing. She could not have had the idea, else how could she have made the petition? And in order to compliment a venerable dame on her pure friendship for a gentleman, it was imperative to reject the idea. Besides, after seeing the photograph of the baroness, common civility insisted on the purity of her friendship. Nay, in mercy to the poor gentleman, friendship it must be.

A letter of reply from that noble lady was due. Possibly she had determined not to write, but to act. She was a lady of exalted birth, a lady of the upper aristocracy, who could, if she would, bring both a social and official pressure upon the General: and it might be in motion now behind the scenes, Clotilde laid hold of her phantom baroness, almost happy under the phantom's whisper that she need not despair. "You have been a little weak," the phantom said to her, and she acquiesced with a soft sniffle, adding: "But, dearest, honoured lady, you are a woman, and know what our trials are when we are so persecuted. O that I had your beautiful sedateness! I do admire it, madam. I wish I could imitate." She carried her dramatic ingenuousness farther still by saying: "I have seen your photograph;" implying that the inimitable, the much coveted air of composure breathed out of yonder presentment of her features. "For I can't call you good-looking," she said within herself, for the satisfaction of her sense of candour, of her sense of contrast as well. And shutting her eyes, she thought of the horrid penitent a harsh-faced woman in confession must be.

The picture sent her swimmingly to the confessional, where sat a man with his head in a hood, and he soon heard enough of mixed substance to dash his hood, almost his head, off. Beauty may be immoderately frank in soul to the ghostly. The black page comprised a very long list. "But put this on the *white* page," says she to the surging father inside his box — "I loved Alvan!" A sentence or two more fetches the Alvanic man jumping out of the priest: and so closely does she realize it that she has to hunt herself into a corner with the question, whether she shall tell him she guessed him to be no other than her lover. "How could you expect a girl, who is not a Papist, to come kneeling here?" she says. And he answers with no matter what of a gallant kind.

In this manner her natural effervescence amused her sorrowful mind while gazing from her chamber window at the mountain sides across the valley, where tourists, in the autumnal season, sweep up and down like a tidal river. She had ceased to weep; she had outwept the colour of her eyes and the consolation of weeping. Dressed in black to the throat, she sat and waited the arrival of her phantom friend, the baroness — that angel! who proved her goodness in consenting to be the friend of Alvan's beloved, because she was the true friend of Alvan! How cheap such a way of proving goodness, Clotilde did not consider. She wanted it so.

The mountain heights were in dusty sunlight. She had seen them day after day thinly lined on the dead sky, inviting thunder and doomed to sultriness. She looked on the garden of the house, a desert under bee and butterfly. Looking beyond the garden she perceived her father on the glaring road, and one with him, the sight of whom did not flush her cheek or spring her heart to a throb, though she pitied the poor boy: — he was useless to her, utterly.

Soon her Indian Bacchus was in the room, and alone with her, and at her feet. Her father had given him hope. He came bearing eyes that were like hope's own; and kneeling, kissing her hands, her knees, her hair, he seemed unaware that she was inanimate.

There was nothing imaginable in which he could be of use.

He was only another dust-cloud of the sultry sameness. She had been expecting a woman, a tempest choral with sky and mountain and valley-hollows, as the overture to Alvan's appearance.

But he roused her. With Marko she had never felt her cowardice, and his passionately beseeching, trembling, "Will you have me?" called up the tiger in the girl; in spite of pity for his voice she retorted on her parents: "Will I have you? I? You ask me what is my will?

It sounds oddly from you, seeing that I wrote to you in Lucerne what I would have, and nothing has changed in me since then, nothing! My feeling for him is unaltered, and everything you have heard of me was wrung out of me by my unhappiness. The world is dead to me, and all in it that is not Sigismund Alvan. To you I am accustomed to speak every thought of my soul, and I tell you the world and all it has is dead to me, even my parents — I hate them."

Marko pressed her hands. If he loved her slavishly, it was generously. The wild thing he said was one of the frantic leaps of generosity in a heart that was gone to impulse: "I see it, they have martyrized you. I know you so well, Clotilde! So, then, come to me, come with me, let me cherish you. I will take you and rescue you from your people, and should it be your positive wish to meet Alvan again, I myself will take you to him, and then you may choose between us."

The generosity was evident. There was nevertheless, to a young woman realizing the position foreshadowed by such a project, the suspicion of a slavish hope nestling among the circumstances in the background, and this she was taught by the dangerous emotion of gratitude gaining on her, and melting her to him.

She too had a slavish hope that was athirst and sinking, and it flew at the throat of Marko's, eager to satiate its vengeance for these long delays in the destroying of a weaker.

She left her chair and cried: "As you will. What is it to me? Take me, if you please. Take that glove; it is the shape of my hand. You have as much of me as is there. My life is gone. You or another! But take this warning and my oath with it. I swear to you, that wherever I see Sigismund Alvan I go straight to him, though the way be over you, all of you, lying dead beneath me."

The lift of incredulous horror in Marko's large black eyes excited her to a more savage imagination: "Rejoice! I should rejoice to see you, all of you, dead, that I might walk across you safe from disturbance to get to him I love. Be under no delusion. I love him better than the lives of any dear to me, or my own. I am his. He is my faith, my worship. I am true to him, I am, I am. You force my hand from me, you take this miserable body, but my soul is free to love him and to go to him when God gives me sight of him. I am Alvan's eternally. All your laws are mockeries. You, and my people, and your priests, and your law-makers, are shadows, brain-vapours. Let him beckon!—So you have your warning. Do what I may, I cannot be called untrue. And now let me be; I want repose; my head breaks; I have been on the rack and I am in pieces!"

Marko clung to her hand, said she was terrible and pitiless, but clung.

The hand was nerveless: it was her dear hand. Had her tongue been more venomous in wildness than the encounter with a weaker than herself made it be, the holding of her hand would have been his antidote. In him there was love for two.

Clotilde allowed him to keep the hand, assuring herself she was unconscious he did so. He brought her peace, he brought her old throning self back to her, and he was handsome and tame as a leopard-skin at her feet.

If she was doomed to reach to Alvan through him, at least she had warned him. The vision of the truthfulness of her nature threw a celestial wan beam on her guilty destiny.

She patted his head and bade him leave her, narrowing her shoulders on the breast to let it be seen that the dark household within was locked and shuttered.

He went. He was good, obedient, humane; he was generous, exquisitely bred; he brought her peace, and he had been warned. It is difficult in affliction to think of one who belongs to us as one to whom we owe a duty. The unquestionably sincere and devoted lover is also in his candour a featureless person; and though we would not punish him for his goodness, we have the right to anticipate that it will be equal to every trial. Perhaps, for the sake of peace . . . after warning him . . . her meditations tottered in dots.

But when the heart hungers behind such meditations, that thinking without language is a dangerous habit; for there will suddenly come a dash usurping the series of tentative dots, which is nothing other than the dreadful thing resolved on, as of necessity, as naturally as the adventurous bow-legged infant pitches back from an excursion of two paces to mother's lap; and not much less innocently within the mind, it would appear. The dash is a haven reached that would not be greeted if it stood out in words. Could we live with ourselves letting our animal do our thinking for us legibly? We live with ourselves agreeably so long as his projects are phrased in his primitive tongue, even though we have clearly apprehended what he means, and though we sufficiently well understand the whither of our destination under his guidance. No counsel can be saner than that the heart should be bidden to speak out in plain verbal speech within us. For want of it, Clotilde's short explorations in Dot-and-Dashland were of a kind to terrify her, and yet they seemed not only unavoidable, but foreshadowing of the unavoidable to come.

Or possibly — the thought came to her — Alvan would keep his word, and save her from worse by stepping to the altar between her and Marko, there calling on her to decide and quit the prince; and his presence would breathe courage into her to go to him. It set her looking to the altar as a prospect of deliverance.

Her mother could not fail to notice a change in Clotilde's wintry face now that Marko was among them; her inference tallied with his report of their interview, so she supposed the girl to have accepted more or less heartily Marko's forgiveness. For him the girl's eyes were soft and kind; her gaze was through the eyelashes, as one seeing a dream on a far horizon. Marko spoke of her cheerfully, and was happy to call her his own, but would not have her troubled by any ceremonial talk of their engagement, so she had much to thank him for, and her consciousness of the signal instance of ingratitude lying ahead in the darkness, like a house mined beneath the smiling slumberer, made her eager to show the real gratefulness and tenderness of her feelings. This had the appearance of renewed affection; consequently her parents lost much of their fear of the besieger outside, and she was removed to the city.

Two parties were in the city, one favouring Alvan, and one abhorring the audacious Jew. Together they managed to spread incredible reports of his doings, which required little exaggeration to convince an enemy that he was a man with whom hostility could not be left to sleep. The General heard of the man's pleading his cause in all directions to get pressure put upon him, showing something like a devilish persuasiveness, Jew and demagogue though he was; for there seemed to be a feeling abroad that the interview this howling lover claimed with Clotilde ought to be granted. The latest report spoke of him as off to the General's Court for an audience of his official chief. General von Rüdiger looked to his defences, and he had sufficient penetration to see that the weakest point of them might be a submissive daughter.

A letter to Clotilde from the baroness was brought to the house by a messenger. The General thought over it. The letter was by no means a seductive letter for a young lady to receive from such a person, yet he did not anticipate the whole effect it would produce when ultimately he decided to give it to her, being of course unaware of the noble style of Clotilde's address to the baroness. He stipulated that there must be no reply to it except through him, and Clotilde had the coveted letter in her hands at last. Here was the mediatrix — the veritable goddess with the sword to cut the knot! Here was the manifestation of Alvan!

## CHAPTER XII.

She ran out to the shade of the garden walls to be by herself and in the air, and she read; and instantly her own letter to the baroness crashed sentence upon sentence, in retort, springing up with the combative instinct of a beast, to make discord of the stuff she read, and deride it. Twice she went over the lines with this defensive accompaniment; then they laid octopus-limbs on her. The writing struck chill as a glacier cave. Oh, what an answer to that letter of fervid respectfulness, of innocent supplication for maternal affection, for some degree of benignant friendship!

The baroness coldly stated, that she had arrived in the city to do her best in assisting to arrange matters, which had come to a most unfortunate and impracticable pass. She alluded to her established friendship for Alvan, but it was chiefly in the interests of Clotilde that the latter was requested to perceive the necessity for bringing her relations with Dr. Alvan to an end in the discreetest manner now possible to the circumstances. This, the baroness pursued, could only be done by her intervention, and her friendship for Dr. Alvan had caused her to undertake the little agreeable office. For which purpose, promising her an exemption from anything in the nature of tragedy scenes, the baroness desired Clotilde to call on her the following day between certain specified hours of the afternoon.

That was all.

The girl in her letter to the baroness had constrained herself to write, and therefore to think, in so beautiful a spirit of ignorant innocence, that the vileness of an answer thus brutally throwing off the mask of personal disinterestedness appeared to her both an abominable piece of cynicism on the part of a scandalous old woman, and an insulting rejection of the cover of decency proposed to the creature by a daisy-minded maiden.

She scribbled a single line in receipt of the letter and signed her initials.

"The woman is hateful!" she said to her father; she was ready to agree with him about the woman and Alvan. She was ashamed to have hoped anything of the woman, and stamped down her disappointment under a vehement indignation, that disfigured the man as well. He had put the matter into the hands of this most detestable of women, to settle it as she might think best! He and she! — the miserable old thing with her ancient arts and cajoleries had lured him back! She had him fast again, in spite of — for who could tell? perhaps by reason of her dirty habits: she smoked dragoon cigars! All day she was emitting tobacco-smoke; it was notorious, Clotilde had not to learn it from her father; but now she saw the filthy rag that standard of female independence was — that petticoated Unfeminine, fouler than masculine! Alvan preferred the lichen-draped tree to the sunny flower, it was evident, for never a letter from Alvan had come to her. She thought in wrath nothing but the thoughts of wrath, and ran her wits through every reasonable reflection like a lighted brand that flings its colour, if not fire, upon surrounding images. Contempt of the square-jawed withered woman was too great for Clotilde to have a sensation of her driving jealousy until painful glimpses of the man made jealousy so sharp that she flew for refuge to contempt of the pair. That beldam had him back: she had him fast. Oh! let her keep him! Was he to be regretted who could make that choice?

Her father did not let the occasion slip to speak insistingly as the world opined of Alvan and his baroness. He forced her to swallow the calumny, and draw away with her family against herself through strong disgust.

Out of a state of fire Clotilde passed into solid frigidity. She had neither a throb nor a passion. Wishing seemed to her senseless as life was. She could hear without a thrill of her frame that Alvan was in the city, without a question whether it was true. He had not written, and he had handed her over to the baroness! She did not ask herself how it was that she had no letter from him, being afraid to think about it, because, if a letter had been withheld by her father, it was a part of her whipping; if none had been written, there was nothing to hope for. Her recent humiliation condemned him by the voice of her sufferings for his failure to be giant, eagle, angel, or any of the prodigious things he had taught her to expect; and as he had thus deceived her, the glorious lover she had imaged in her mind was put aside with some of the angry disdain she bestowed upon the woman by whom she had been wounded. He ceased to be a visioned Alvan, and became an obscurity; her principal sentiment in relation to him was, that he threatened her peace. But for him she would never have been taught to hate her parents; she would have enjoyed the quiet domestic evenings with her people, when Marko sang, and her sisters knitted, and the betrothed sister wore a look very enviable in the abstract; she would be seeing a future instead of a black iron gate! But for him she certainly would never have had that letter from the baroness!

On the morning after the information of Alvan's return, her father, who deserved credit as a tactician, came to her to say that Alvan had sent to demand his letters and presents. The demand was unlike what her stunned heart recollected of Alvan; but a hint that the baroness was behind it, and that a refusal would bring the baroness down on her with another piece of insolence, was effective. She dealt out the letters, arranged the presents, made up the books, pamphlets, trinkets, amulet coins, lock of black hair, and worn post-marked paper addressed in his hand to Clotilde von Rüdiger, carefully; and half as a souvenir, half with the forlorn yearning of the look of lovers when they break asunder — or of one of them — she signed inside the packet not "Clotilde," but the gentlest title he had bestowed on her, trusting to the pathos of the word "child" to tell him that she was enforced and still true, if he should be interested in knowing it. Weak souls are much moved by having the pathos on their side. They are consoled too.

Time passed, whole days: the tender reminder had no effect on him! It had been her last appeal: she reflected that she had really felt when he had not been feeling at all: and this marks a division.

She was next requested to write a letter to Alvan, signifying his release by the notification of her engagement to Prince Marko. She was personally to deliver it to a gentleman who was of neither party, and who would give her a letter from Alvan in exchange, which, while assuring the gentleman she was acting with perfect freedom, she was to be under her oath not to read, and dutifully to hand to Marko, her betrothed. Her father assumed the fact of her renewed engagement to the prince, as her whole family did; strangely, she thought: it struck her as a fatality. He said that Alvan was working him great mischief, doing him deadly injury in his position, and for no just reason, inasmuch as he — a bold, bad man striving to ruin the family on a point of pride — had declared that he simply considered himself bound in honour to her, only a little doubtful of her independent action at present; and a release of him, accompanied by her plain statement of her being under no compulsion, voluntarily the betrothed of another, would solve the difficulty. A certain old woman, it seemed, was anxious to have him formally released.

With the usual dose for such a patient, of cajoleries and threats, the General begged her to comply, pulling the hands he squeezed in a way to strongly emphasize his affectionate entreaty.

She went straight to Marko, consenting that he should have Alvan's letter unopened (she cared not to read it, she said), on his promise to give it up to her within a stated period. There was a kind of prohibited pleasure, sweet acid, catching discord, in the idea of this lover's keeping the forbidden thing she could ask for when she was curious about the other, which at present she was not; dead rather; anxious to please her parents, and determined to be no rival of the baroness. Marko promised it readily, adding: "Only let the storm roll over, that we may have more liberty, and I myself, when we two are free, will lead you to Alvan, and leave it to you to choose between us. Your happiness, beloved, is my sole thought. Submit for the moment." He spoke sweetly, with his dearest look, touching her luxurious nature with a belief that she could love him; untroubled by another, she could love and be true to him: her maternal inner nature yearned to the frail-bodied youth.

She made a comparison in her mind of Alvan's love and Marko's, and of the lives of the two men. There was no grisly baroness attached to the prince's life.

She wrote the letter to Alvan, feeling in the words that said she was plighted to Prince Marko, that she said, and clearly said, the baroness is now relieved of a rival, and may take you! She felt it so acutely as to feel that she said nothing else.

Severances are accomplished within the heart stroke by stroke; within the craven's heart each new step resulting from a blow is temporarily an absolute severance. Her letter to Alvan written, she thought not tenderly of him but of the prince, who had always loved a young woman, and was unhampered by an old one. The composition of the letter, and the sense that the thing was done, made her stony to Alvan.

On the introduction of Colonel von Tresten, whose name she knew, but was dull to it, she delivered him her letter with unaffected composure, received from him Alvan's in exchange, left the room as if to read it, and after giving it unopened to Marko, composedly reappeared before the colonel to state, that the letter could make no difference, and all was to be as she had written it.

The colonel bowed stiffly.

It would have comforted her to have been allowed to say: "I cease to be the rival of that execrable harridan!"

The delivery of so formidable a cat-screech not being possible, she stood in an attitude of mild resignation, revolving thoughts of her father's praises of his noble daughter, her mother's kiss, the caresses of her sisters, and the dark bright eyes of Marko, the peace of the domestic circle. This was her happiness! And still there was time, still hope for Alvan to descend and cut the knot. She conceived it slowly, with some flush of the brain like a remainder of fever, but no throbs of her pulses. She had been swayed to act against him by tales which in her heart she did not credit exactly, therefore did not take within herself, though she let them influence her by the goad of her fears and angers; and these she could conjure up at will for the defence of her conduct, aware of their shallowness, and all the while trusting him to come in the end and hear her reproaches for his delay. He seemed to her now to have the character of a storm outside a household wrapped in comfortable monotony. Her natural spiritedness detested the monotony, her craven soul fawned for the comfort. After her many recent whippings the comfort was immensely desirable, but a glance at the monotony gave it the look of a burial, and standing in her attitude of resignation under Colonel von Tresten's hard military stare she could have shrieked for Alvan to come, knowing that she would have cowered and trembled at the scene following his appearance. Yet she would have gone to him; without any doubt his presence and the sense of his greater power declared by his coming would have lifted her over to him. The part of her nature adoring storminess wanted only a present champion to outweigh the other part which cuddled security. Colonel von Tresten, however, was very far from offering himself in such a shape to a girl that had jilted the friend he loved, insulted the woman he esteemed; and he stood there like a figure of soldierly complacency in marble. Her pencilled acknowledgment of the baroness's letter, and her reply to it almost as much, was construed as an intended insult to that lady, whose champion Tresten was. He had departed before Clotilde heard a step.

Immediately thereupon it came to her mind that Tresten was one of Alvan's bosom friends. How, then, could he be of neither party? And her father spoke of him as an upright rational man, who, although, strangely enough, he entertained, as it appeared, something like a profound reverence for the baroness, could see and confess the downright impossibility of the marriage Alvan proposed. Tresten, her father said, talked of his friend Alvan as wild and eccentric, but now becoming convinced that such a family as hers could never tolerate him — considering his age, his birth, his blood, his habits, his politics, his private entanglements and moral reputation, it was partly hinted.

She shuddered at this false Tresten. He and the professor might be strung together for examples of perfidy! His reverence of the baroness gave his cold blue eyes the iciness of her loathed letter. Alvan, she remembered, used to exalt him among the gallantest of the warriors dedicating their swords to freedom. The dedication of the sword, she felt sure, was an accident: he was a man of blood. And naturally, she must be hated by the man reverencing the baroness. If ever man had *executioner* stamped on his face, it was he! Like the professor, nay, like Alvan himself, he would not see that she was the victim of tyranny: none of her signs would they see. They judged of her by her inanimate frame in the hands of her torturers breaking her on the wheel. She called to mind a fancy that she had looked at Tresten out of her deadness earnestly for just one instant: more than an instant she could not, beneath her father's vigilant watch and into those repellant cold blue butcher eyes. Tresten might clearly have understood the fleeting look. What were her words! what her deeds! The look was the truth revealed — her soul. It begged for life like an infant; and the man's face was an iron rock in reply! No wonder he worshipped the baroness! So great was Clotilde's hatred of him that it overflooded the image of Alvan, who called him friend, and deputed him to act as friend. Such blindness, weakness, folly, on the part of one of Alvan's pretensions, incurred a shade of her contempt. She had not ever thought of him coldly: hitherto it would have seemed a sacrilege; but now she said definitely, the friend of Tresten cannot be the man I supposed him! and she ascribed her capacity for saying it, and for perceiving and adding up Alvan's faults of character, to the freezing she had taken from that most antipathetic person. She confessed to sensations of spite which would cause her to reject and spurn even his pleadings for Alvan, if they were imaginable as actual. Their not being imaginable allowed her to indulge her naughtiness harmlessly, for the gratification of the idea of wounding some one, though it were her lover, connected with this Tresten.

The letter of the baroness and the visit of the woman's admirer had vitiated Clotilde's blood. She was not only not mistress of her thoughts, she was undirected either in thinking or wishing by any desires, except that the people about her should caress and warm her, until, with no gaze backward, she could say good-bye to them, full of meaning as a good-bye to the covered grave, as unreluctantly as the swallow quits her eaves-nest in autumn: and they were to learn that they were chargeable with the sequel of the history. There would be a sequel, she was sure, if it came only to punish them for the cruelty which thwarted her timid anticipation of it by pressing on her natural instinct at all costs to bargain for an escape from pain, and making her simulate contentment to cheat her muffled wound and them.

## CHAPTER XIII.

His love meantime was the mission and the burden of Alvan, and he was not ashamed to speak of it and plead for it; and the pleading was not done troubadourishly, in soft flute-notes, as for easement of tuneful emotions beseeching sympathy. He was liker to a sturdy beggar demanding his crust, to support life, of corporations that can be talked into admitting the rights of man; and he vollied close logical argumentation, on the basis of the laws, in defence of his most natural hunger, thunder in his breast and bright new heavenly morning alternating or clashing while the electric wires and post smote him with evil tidings of Clotilde, and the success of his efforts caught her back to him. Daily many times he reached to her and lost her, had her in his arms and his arms withered with emptiness. The ground he won quaked under him. All the evidence opposed it, but he was in action, and his reason swore that he had her fast. He had seen and felt his power over her; his reason told him by what had been that it must be. Could he doubt? He battled for his reason. Doubt was an extinguishing wave, and he clung to his book of the Law, besieging Church and State with it, pointing to texts of the law which proved her free to choose her lord and husband for herself, expressing his passionate love by his precise interpretation of the law: and still with the cold sentience gaining on him, against the current of his tumultuous blood and his hurried intelligence, of her being actually what he had named her in moments of playful vision — slippery, a serpent, a winding hare; with the fear that she might slip from him, betray, deny him, deliver him to ridicule, after he had won his way to her over every barrier. During his proudest exultations in success, when his eyes were sparkling, there was a wry twitch inward upon his heart of hearts.

But if she was a hare, he was a hunter, little inclining to the chase now for mere physical recreation. She had roused the sportsman's passion as well as the man's; he meant to hunt her down, and was not more scrupulous than our ancient hunters, who hunted for a meal and hunted to kill, with none of the later hesitations as to circumventing, trapping, snaring by devices, and the preservation of the animal's coat spotless. Let her be lured from her home, or plucked from her home, and if reluctant, disgraced, that she may be dependent utterly on the man stooping to pick her up! He was equal to the projecting of a scheme socially infamous, with such fanatical intensity did the thought of his losing the woman harass him, and the torrent of his passion burst restraint to get to her to enfold her — this in the same hour of the original wild monster's persistent and sober exposition of the texts of the law with the voice of a cultivated modern gentleman; and, let it be said, with a modern gentleman's design to wed a wife in honour. All means were to be tried. His eye burned on his prize, mindless of what she was dragged through, if there was resistance, or whether by the hair of her head or her skirts, or how she was obtained. His interpretation of the law was for the powers of earth, and other plans were to propitiate the powers under the earth, and certain distempered groanings wrenched from him at intervals he addressed (after they were out of him, reflectively) to the powers above, so that nothing of him should be lost which might get aid of anything mundane, infernal, or celestial.

Thus is it when Venus bites a veritable ancient male. She puts her venom in a magnificent beast, not a pathetic Phaedra. She does it rarely, for though to be loved by a bitten giant is one of the dreams of woman, the considerate Mother of Love knows how needful it is to protect the sentiment of the passion and save them from an exhibition of the fires of that dragon's breath. Do they not fly shrieking when they behold it? Barely are they able to read of it. Men, too, accustomed to minor doses of the goddess, which moderate, soften, counteract, instead of inflicting the malady, abhor and have no brotherhood with its turbulent victim.

It was justly matter for triumph, due to an extraordinary fervour of pleading upon a plain statement of the case, that Alvan should return from his foray bringing with him an emissary deputed by General von Rüdiger's official chief to see that the young lady, so passionately pursued by the foremost of his time in political genius and oratory, was not subjected to parental tyranny, but stood free to exercise her choice. Of the few who would ever have thought of attempting, a diminished number would have equalled that feat. Alvan was no vain boaster; he could gain the ears of grave men as well as mobs and women. The interview with Clotilde was therefore assured to him, and the distracting telegrams and letters forwarded to him by Tresten during his absence were consequently stabs already promising to heal. They were brutal stabs: her packet of his letters and presents on his table made them bleed afresh, and the odd scrawl of the couple of words on the paper set him wondering at the imbecile irony of her calling herself "The child" in accompaniment to such an act, for it reminded him of his epithet for her, while it dealt him a tremendous blow; it seemed senselessly malign, perhaps flippant, as she could be, he knew. She could be anything weak and shallow when out of his hands; she had recently proved it: still, in view of the interview, and on the tide of his labours to come to that wished end, he struck his breast to brave himself with a good hopeful spirit. "Once mine!" he said.

Moreover, to the better account, Clotilde's English friend had sent him the lines addressed to her, in which the writer dwelt on her love of him with a whimper of the voice of love. That was previous to her perjury: by little, by a day — eighteen hours. How lurid a satire was flung on events by the proximity of the dates! But the closeness of the time between this love-crooning and the denying of him pointed to a tyrannous intervention. One could detect it. Full surely the poor craven was being tyrannized and tutored to deny him! though she was a puss of the fields too, as the mounted sportsman was not unwilling to think.

Before visiting his Mentor, Alvan applied for an audience of General von Rüdiger, who granted it at once to a man coming so well armed to claim the privilege. Tresten walked part of the way to the General's house with him, and then turned aside to visit the baroness.

Lucie, Baroness von **Crefeldt,** was one of those persons

who, after a probationary term in the character of woman, have become men, but of whom offended man, amazed by the flowering up of that hard rough jaw from the tender blooming promise of a petticoat, finds it impossible to imagine they had once on a sweet Spring time the sex's gentleness and charm of aspect. Mistress Flanders, breeched and hatted like a man, pulling at the man's short pipe and heartily invoking frouzy deities, committing a whole sackful of unfeminine etcætera, is an impenetrable wall to her maiden past; yet was there an opening day when nothing of us moustached her. She was a clear-faced girl and mother of young blushes before the years were at their work of transformation upon her countenance and behind her bosom. The years were rough artists: perhaps she was combative, and fought them for touching her ungallantly; and that perhaps was her first manly step. Baroness Lucie was of high birth, a wife openly maltreated, a woman of breeding, but with a man's head, capable of inspiring man-like friendships, and of entertaining them. She was radically-minded, strongly of the Radical profession of faith, and a correspondent of revolutionary chiefs; both the trusted adviser and devoted slave of him whose future glorious career she measured by his abilities. Rumour blew out a candle and left the wick to smoke in relation to their former intercourse. The Philistines revenged themselves on an old aristocratic Radical and a Jew demagogue with the weapon that scandal hands to virtue. They are virtuous or nothing, and they must show that they are so when they can; and best do they show it by publicly dishonouring the friendship of a man and a woman; for to be in error in malice does not hurt them, but they profoundly feel that they are fools if they are duped.

She was aware of the recent course of events; she had, as she protested, nothing to accuse herself of, and she could hardly part her lips without a self-exculpation.

"It will fall on me!" she said to Tresten, in her emphatic tone. "He will have his interview with the girl. He will subdue the girl. He will manacle himself in the chains he makes her wear. She will not miss her chance! I am the object of her detestation. I am the price paid for their reconcilement. She will seize her opportunity to vilipend me, and I shall be condemned by the kind of court-martial which hurries over the forms of a trial to sign the execution-warrant that makes it feel like justice. You will see. She cannot forgive me for not pretending to enter into her enthusiasm. She will make him believe I conspired against her. Men in love are children with their mistresses — the greatest of them; their heads are under the woman's feet. What have I not done to aid him! At his instance, I went to the archbishop, to implore one of the princes of the Church for succour. I knelt to an ecclesiastic. I did a ludicrous and a shameful thing, knowing it in advance to be a barren farce. I obeyed his wish. The tale will be laughable. I obeyed him. I would not have it on my conscience that the commission of any deed ennomic, however unwonted, was refused by me to serve Alvan. You are my witness, Tresten, that for a young woman of common honesty I was ready to pack and march. Qualities of mind — mind! They were out of the question. He had a taste for a wife. If he had hit on a girl commonly honest, she might not have harmed him — the contrary; cut his talons. What is this girl? Exactly what one might be sure his appreciation, in woman-flesh, would lead him to fix on; a daughter of the Philistines, naturally, and precisely the one of all on earth likely to confound him after marriage as she has played fast and loose with him before it. He has never understood women — cannot read them. Could a girl like that keep a secret? She's a Cressida — a creature of every camp! Not an idea of the cause he is vowed to! not a sentiment in harmony with it! She is viler than any of those Berlin light o' loves on the eve of Jena. Stable as a Viennese dancing slut home from Mariazell! This is the girl — transparent to the whole world! But his heart is on her, and he must have her, I suppose; and I shall have to bear her impertinences, or sign my demission and cease to labour for the cause — at least in conjunction with Alvan. And how otherwise? He is the life of it, and I am doomed to uselessness."

Tresten nodded a protesting assent.

"Not quite so bad," he said, with the encouraging smile

which would persuade a friend to put away bilious visions.
"Of the two, if you two are divisible, we could better
dispense with him. She'll slip him, she's an eel. I
have seen eels twine on a prong of the fork that prods
them; but she's an actress, a slippery one through and
through, with no real embrace in her, not even a common
muscular contraction. Of every camp! as you say. She
was not worth carrying off. I consented to try it to quiet
him. He sets no bounds to his own devotion to friendship,
and we must take pattern by him. It's a mad love."

"A Titan's love!" the baroness exclaimed, groaning.
"The woman! — no matter how or at what cost! I can
admire that primal barbarism of a great man's passion,
which counts for nothing the stains and accidents fraught
with extinction for it to meaner men. It reads ill, it
sounds badly, but there is grand stuff in it. See the royalty
of the man, for whom no degradation of the woman can
be, so long as it brings her to him! He — that great *he* —
covers all. He burns her to ashes, and takes the flame —
the pure spirit of her — to himself. Were men like him!
— they would have less to pardon. We must, as I have
ever said, be morally on alpine elevations to comprehend
Alvan; he is Mont Blanc above his fellows. Do not ask
him to be considerate of her. She has planted him in a
storm, and the bigger the mountain, the more savage,
monstrous, cruel — yes, but *she* blew up the tourmente!
That girl is the author of his madness. It is the snake's
nature of the girl which distracts him; she is in his blood.
Had she come to me, I would have helped her to cure
him; or had you succeeded in carrying her off, I would
have stood by their union; or were she a different creature,
and not the shifty thing she is, I could desire him to win
her. A peasant girl, a workman's daughter, a trades-
man's, a professional singer, actress, artist — I would have
given my hand to one of these in good faith, thankful to
her! As it is, I have acted in obedience to his wishes,
without idle remonstrances — I know him too well; and
with as much cordiality as I could put into an evil service.
She will drag him down, down, Tresten!"

"They are not joined yet," said the colonel.

"She has him by the worst half of him. Her correspondence with me — her letter to excuse her insolence, which she does like a prim chit — throws a light on the girl she is. She will set him aiming at power to trick her out in the decorations. She will not keep him to his labours to consolidate the power. She will pervert the æsthetic in him, through her hold on his material nature, his vanity, his luxuriousness. She is one of the young women who begin timidly, and when they see that they enjoy comparative impunity, grow intrepid in dissipation, and that palling, they are ravenously ambitious. She will drive him at his mark before the time is ripe — ruin him. He is a Titan, not a god, though god-like he seems in comparison with men. He would be fleshly enough in any hands. This girl will drain him of all his nobler fire."

"She shows mighty little of the inclination," said the colonel.

"To you. But when they come together? I know his voice!"

The colonel protested his doubts of their coming together.

"Ultimately?" the baroness asked, and brooded. "But she will have to see him; and then will she resist him? I shall change one view of her if she does."

"She will shirk the interview," Tresten remarked. "Supposing they meet: I don't think much will come of it, unless they meet on a field, and he has an hour's grace to catch her up and be off with her. She's as calm as the face of a clock, and wags her Yes and No about him just as unconcernedly as a clock's pendulum. I've spoken to many a sentinel outpost who wasn't deader on the subject in monosyllables than mademoiselle. She has a military erectness, and answers you and looks you straight at the eyes, perfectly unabashed by you seeing 'the girl she is,' as you say. She looked at me downright defying me to despise her. Alvan has been tricked by her colour: she's icy. She has no passion. She acts up to him when they're together, and that deceives him. I doubt her having blood — there's no heat in it, if she has."

"And he cajoled Count Hollinger to send an envoy to see him righted!" the baroness ejaculated. "Hollinger is not a sentimental person, I assure you, and not likely to have taken a step apparently hostile to the Rüdigers, if he had not been extraordinarily shaken by Alvan. What character of man is this Dr. Störchel?"

Tresten described Count Hollinger's envoy, so quaintly deputed to act the part of legal umpire in a family business, as a mild man of law with no ideas or interests outside the law; spectacled, nervous, formal, a stranger to the passions; and the baroness was amused to hear of Störchel and Alvan's placid talk together upon themes of law, succeeded by the little advocate's bewildered fright at one of Alvan's gentler explosions. Tresten sketched it. The baroness realized it, and shut her lips tight for a laugh of essential humour.

## CHAPTER XIV.

LATE in the day Alvan was himself able to inform her that he had overcome Clotilde's father after a struggle of hours. The General had not consented to everything: he had granted enough, evidently in terror of the man who had captured Count Hollinger; and it was arranged that Tresten and Störchel were to wait on Clotilde next morning, and hear from her mouth whether she yielded or not to Alvan's request to speak with her alone before the official interview in the presence of the notary, when she was publicly to state her decision and freedom of choice, according to Count Hollinger's amicable arrangement through his envoy.

"She will see me — and the thing is done!" said Alvan. "But I have worked for it — I have worked! I have been talking to-day for six hours uninterruptedly at a stretch to her father, who reminds me of a caged bear I saw at a travelling menagerie, and the beast would perform none of his evolutions for the edification of us lads till his keeper touched a particular pole, and the touch of it set him to work like the winding of a key. Hollinger's name was my magic wand with the General. I could get no sense from him, nor any acquiescence in sense, till I called up Hollinger, when the General's alacrity was immediately that of the bear, or a little boy castigated for his share of original sin. They have been hard at her, the whole family! and I shall want the two hours I stipulated for to the full. What do you say? — come, I wager I do it within one hour! They have stockaded her pretty closely, and it will be some time before I shall get her to have a clear view of me behind her defences; but an hour's an age with a woman. Clotilde? I wager I have her on her knees in half an hour! These notions of duty, and station, and her fiddle-de-dee betrothal to that Danube osier with Indian-idol eyes, count for so much mist. She was and is mine. I swear to strike to her heart in ten minutes! But, madam, if not, you may pronounce me incapable of conquering any woman, or of taking an absolute impression of facts. I say I will do it! I am insane if I may not judge from antecedents that my voice, my touch, my face, will draw her to me at one signal — at a look! I am prepared to stake my reason on her running to me before I speak a word: — and I will not beckon. I promise to fold my arms and simply look."

"Your task of two hours, then, will be accomplished, I compute, in about half a minute — but it is on the assumption that she consents to see you alone," said the baroness.

Alvan opened his eyes. He perceived in his deep sagaciousness woman at the bottom of her remark, and replied: "You will know Clotilde in time. She points to me straight; but of course if you agitate the compass the needle's all in a tremble: and the vessel is weak, I admit, but the instinct's positive. To doubt it would upset my understanding. I have had three distinct experiences of my influence over her, and each time, curiously each time exactly in proportion to *my* degree of resolve — but, baroness, I tell you it was *minutely* in proportion to it; weighed down to the grain! — each time did that girl respond to me with a similar degree of earnestness. As I waned she waned; as I heated, so did she, and from spark-heat to flame and to furnace-heat!"

"A refraction of the rays according to the altitude of the orb," observed the baroness in a tone of assent, and she smiled to herself at the condition of the man who could accept it for that.

He did not protest beyond presently a transient frown as at a bad taste on his tongue, and a rather petulant objection to her use of analogies, which he called the sapping of language. She forbore to remind him in retort of his employment of metaphor when the figure served his purpose.

"Marvellously," cried Alvan, "marvellously that girl answered to my lead! and to-morrow — you'll own me right — I must double the attraction. I shall have to hand her back to her people for twenty-four hours, and the dose must be doubled to keep her fast and safe. You see I read her flatly. I read and am charitable. I have a perfect philosophical tolerance. I'm in the mood to-day of Horace hymning one of his fair Greeks."

"No, no! that is a comparison past my endurance," interposed the baroness. "Friend Sigismund, you have no philosophy, you never had any; and the small crow and croon of Horace would be the last you could take up. It is the chanted philosophy of comfortable stipendiaries, retired merchants, gouty patients on a restricted allowance of the grape, old men who have given over thinking, and young men who never had feeling — the philosophy of swine grunting their carmen as they turn to fat in the sun. Horace avaunt! You have too much poetry in you to quote that unsanguine sensualist for your case. His love distressed his liver, and gave him a jaundice once or twice, but where his love yields its poor ghost to his philosophy, yours begins its labours. That everlasting Horace! He is the versifier of the cushioned enemy, not of us who march along flinty ways: the piper of the bourgeois in soul, poet of the conforming unbelievers!"

"Pyrrha, Lydia, Lalage, Chloe, Glycera," Alvan murmured, amorous of the musical names. "Clotilde is a Greek of one of the Isles, an Ionian. I see her in the Horatian ode as in one of those old round shield-mirrors which give you a speck of the figure on a silver-solar beam, brilliant, not much bigger than a dewdrop. And so should a man's heart reflect her! Take her on the light in it, she is perfection. We won't take her in the shady part or on your flat looking-glasses. There never was necessity for accuracy of line in the portraiture of women. The idea of them is all we want: it's the best of them. You will own she's Greek; she's a Perinthian, Andrian, Olynthian, Samian, Messenian. One of those delicious girls in the New

Comedy, I remember, was called THE POSTPONER, THE DEFERRER, or, as we might say, THE TO-MORROWER. There you have Clotilde: she's a TO-MORROWER. You climb the peak of to-morrow, and to see her at all you must see her on the next peak: but she leaves you her promise to hug on every yesterday, and that keeps you going. Ay, so long as we have patience! Feeding on a young woman's promises of yesterday in one's fortieth year! — it must end to-morrow, though I kill something."

Kill, he meant, the aërial wild spirit he could admire as her character, when he had the prospect of extinguishing it in his grasp.

"What do you meditate killing?" said the baroness.

"The fool of the years behind me," he replied, "and entering on my forty-first a sage."

"To be the mate and equal of your companion?"

"To prove I have had good training under the wisest to act as her guide and master."

"If she —— " the baroness checked her exclamation, saying: "She declined to come to me. I would have plumbed her for some solid ground, something to rest one's faith on. Your Pyrrhas, Glyceras, and others of the like, were not stable persons for a man of our days to bind his life to one of them. Harness is harness, and a light yoke-fellow can make a proud career deviate."

"But I give her a soul!" said Alvan. "I am the wine, and she the crystal cup. She has avowed it again and again. You read her as she is when away from me. Then she is a reed, a weed, what you will; she is unfit to contend when she stands alone. But when I am beside her, when we are together — the moment I have her at arms' length she will be part of me by the magic I have seen each time we encountered. She knows it well."

"She may know it too well."

"For what?" He frowned.

"For the chances of your meeting."

"You think it possible she will refuse?"

A blackness passing to lividness crossed his face. He fetched a big breath.

"Then finish my history, shut up the book; I am a phantom of a man, and everything written there is imposture! I can account for all that she has done hitherto, but not that she should refuse to see me. Not that she should refuse to see me now when I come armed to demand it! Refuse? But I have done my work, done what I said I would do. I stand in my order of battle, and she refuses? No! I stake my head on it! I have not a clod's perception, I have not a spark of sense to distinguish me from a flat-headed Lapp, if she refuses: — call me a mountebank who has gained his position by clever tumbling; a lucky gamester; whatever plays blind with chance."

He started up in agitation. "Lucie! I am a grinning skull without a brain if that girl refuses! She will not." He took his hat to leave, adding, to seem rational to the cool understanding he addressed: " She will not refuse; I am bound to think so in common respect for myself; I have done tricks to make me appear a rageing ape if she — oh! she cannot, she will not refuse. Never! I have eyes, I have wits, I am not tottering yet on my grave — or it's blindly, if I am. I have my clear judgement, I am not an imbecile. It seems to me a foolish suspicion that she can possibly refuse. Her manners are generally good; freakish, but good in the main. Perhaps she takes a sting . . . but there is no sting here. It would be bad manners to refuse; — to say nothing of . . . she has a heart! Well, then, good manners and right feeling forbid her to refuse. She is an exceedingly intelligent girl, and I half fear I have helped you to a wrong impression of her. You will really appreciate her wit; you will indeed; believe me, you will. We pardon nonsense in a girl. Married, she will put on the matron with becoming decency, and I am responsible for her then; I stand surety for her then; when I have her with me I warrant her mine and all mine, head and heels, at a whistle, like the Cossack's horse. I fancy that at forty I am about as young as most young men. I promise her another forty manful working years. Are you dubious of that?"

"I nod to you from the palsied summit of ninety," said the baroness.

Alvan gave a short laugh and stammered excuses for his naked egoism, comparing himself to a forester who has sharpened such an appetite in toiling to slay his roe that he can think of nothing but the fire preparing the feast.

"Hymen and things hymenæal!" he said, laughing at himself for resuming the offence on the apology for it. "I could talk with interest of a trousseau. I have debated in my mind with parliamentary acrimony about a choice of wedding-presents. As she is legally free to bestow her hand on me — and only a brute's horns could contest the fact — she may decide to be married the day after tomorrow, and get the trousseau in Paris. She has a turn for startling. I can imagine that if I proposed a run for it she would be readier to spring to be on the road with me than in acquiescing in a quiet arrangement about a ceremonial day; partly because, in the first case, she would throw herself and the rest of the adventure on me, at no other cost than the enjoyment of one of her impulses; and in the second, because she is a girl who would require a full band of the best Berlin orchestra in perpetual play to keep up her spirits among her people during the preparations for espousing a democrat, demagogue, and Jew, of a presumed inferior station by birth to her own. Give Momus a sister, Clotilde is the lady! I know her. I would undertake to put a spell on her and keep her contented on a frontier — not Russian, any barbarous frontier where there is a sun. She must have sun. One might wrap her in sables, but sun is best. She loves it best, though she looks remarkably well in sables. Never shall I forget . . . she is *frileuse*, and shivers into them! There are Frenchmen who could paint it — only Frenchmen. Our artists, no. She is very French. Born in France she would have been a matchless Parisienne. Oh! she's a riddle of course. I don't pretend to spell every letter of her. The returning of my presents is odd. No, I maintain that she is a coward acting under domination, and there's no other way of explaining the puzzle. I was out of sight, they bullied her, and she yielded — bewilderingly, past comprehension it seems — cat! — until you remember what she's made of: she's a reed. Now I reappear armed with powers to give her a free course, and she, *that abject* whom you beheld recently renouncing me, is, you will see, the young Aurora she was when she came striking at my door on the upper Alp.

That was a morning! That morning is Clotilde till my eyes turn over! She is all young heaven and the mountains for me! She's the filmy light above the mountains that weds white snow and sky. By the way, I dreamt last night she was half a woman, half a tree, and her hair was like a dead yew-bough, which is as you know of a brown burnt-out colour, suitable to the popular conception of widows. She stood, and whatever turning you took, you struck back on her. Whether *my* widow, I can't say: she must first be my wife. Oh, for to-morrow!"

"What sort of evening is it?" said the baroness.

"A Mont Blanc evening: I saw him as I came along," Alvan replied, and seized his hat to be out to look on the sovereign mountain again. They touched hands. He promised to call in the forenoon next day.

"Be cool," she counselled him.

"Oh!" He flung back his head, making light of the crisis. "After all, it's only a girl. But, you know, what I set myself to win! . . . The thing's too small — I have been at such pains about it that I should be ridiculous if I allowed myself to be beaten. There is no other reason for the trouble we're at, except that, as I have said a thousand times, she suits me. No man can be cooler than I."

"Keep so," said the baroness.

He walked to where the strenuous blue lake, finding outlet, propels a shoulder, like a bright-muscled athlete in action, and makes the Rhone-stream. There he stood for an hour, disfevered by the limpid liquid tumult, inspirited by the glancing volumes of a force that knows no abatement, and is the skiey Alps behind, the great historic citied plains ahead.

His meditation ended with a resolution half in the form of a prayer (to mixed deities undefined) never to ask for a small thing any more if this one were granted him!

He had won it, of course, having brought all his powers to bear on the task; and he rejoiced in winning it: his heart leapt, his imagination spun radiant webs of colour: but he was a little ashamed of his frenzies, though he did not distinctly recall them; he fancied he had made some noise, loud or not, because his intentions were so pure that it was infamous to thwart them. At a certain age honest men made sacrifice of their liberty to society, and he had been ready to perform the duty of husbanding a woman. A man should have a wife and rear children, not to be forgotten in the land, and to help mankind by transmitting to future times qualities he has proved priceless : he thought of the children, and yearned to the generations of men physically and morally through them.

This was his apology to the world for his distantly-recollected excesses of temper.

Was she so small a thing? Not if she succumbed. She was petty, vexatious, irritating, stinging, while she resisted: she cast an evil beam on his reputation, strength and knowledge of himself, and roused the giants of his nature to discharge missiles at her, justified as they were by his pure intentions and the approbation of society. But he had a broad full heart for the woman who would come to him, forgiving her, uplifting her, richly endowing her. No meanness of heart was in him. He lay down at night thinking of Clotilde in an abandonment of tenderness. "To-morrow! you bird of to-morrow!" he let fly his good-night to her.

## CHAPTER XV.

HE slept. Near upon morning he roused with his tender fit strong on him, but speechless in the waking as it had been dreamless in sleep. It was a happy load on his breast, a life about to be born, and he thought that a wife beside him would give it language. She should have, for she would call out, his thousand flitting ideas now dropped on barren ground for want of her fair bosom to inspire, to vivify, to receive. Poetry laid a hand on him: his desire of the wife, the children, the citizen's good name — of these our simple civilized ambitions — was lowly of the earth, throbbing of earth, and at the same time magnified beyond scope of speech in vast images and emblems resembling ranges of Olympian cloud round the blue above earth, all to be decipherable, all utterable, when she was by. What commoner word! — yet *wife* seemed to him the word most reverberating of the secret sought after by man, fullest at once of fruit and of mystery, or of that light in the heart of mystery which makes it magically fruitful.

He felt the presence of Clotilde behind the word; but in truth the delicate sensations breeding these half-thoughts of his, as he lay between sleeping and waking, shrank from conjuring up the face of the woman who had wounded them, and a certain instinct to preserve and be sure of his present breathing-space of luxurious tranquillity kept her veiled. Soon he would see her as his wife, and then she would be she, unveiled ravishingly, the only she, the only wife! He knew the cloud he clasped for Clotilde enough to be at pains to shun a possible prospect of his execrating it. Oh, the only she, the only wife! the wild man's reclaimer! the sweet abundant valley and channel of his river of existence henceforward! Doubting her in the slightest was doubting her human. It is the brain, the satanic brain which will ever be pressing to cast its shadows: the heart is clearer and truer.

He multiplied images, projected visions, nestled in his throbs to drug and dance his brain. He snatched at the beauty of a day that outrolled the whole Alpine hand-in-hand of radiant heaven-climbers for an assurance of predestined celestial beneficence; and again, shadowily thoughtful of the littleness of the thing he exalted and claimed, he staked his reason on the positive blessing to come to him before nightfall, telling himself calmly that he did so because there would be madness in expecting it otherwise: he asked for so little! Since he asked for so little, to suppose that it would not be granted was irrational. None but a very coward could hesitate to stake his all on the issue.

Singularly small indeed the other aims in life appeared by comparison with this one, but his intellect, in the act of pleading excuses for his impatience, distinguished why it should be so. The crust, which is not much, is everything to the starving beggar; and he was eager for the crust that he might become sound and whole again, able to give their just proportion to things, as at present he acknowledged himself hardly able to do. He could not pursue two thoughts on a political question, or grasp the idea of a salutary energy in the hosts animated by his leadership

There would have to be an end of it speedily, else men might name him worthless dog!

Morning swam on the lake in her beautiful nakedness, a wedding of white and blue, of purest white and bluest blue. Alvan crossed the island bridges when the sun had sprung on his shivering fair prey, to make the young fresh Morning rosy, and was glittering along the smooth lake-waters. Workmen only were abroad, and Alvan was glad to be out with them to feel with them as one of them. Close beside him the vivid genius of the preceding century, whose love of workmen was a salt of heaven in his human corruptness, looked down on the lake in marble. Alvan cherished a worship of him as of one that had first thrilled him with the feeling of our common humanity, with the tenderness for the poor, with the knowledge of our frailty. Him, as well as the great Englishman and a Frenchman, his mind called Father, and his conscience replied to that progenitor's questioning of him, but said "You know the love of woman." He loved indeed, but he was not an amatory trifler. He too was a worker, a champion worker. He doated on the prospect of plunging into his work; the vision of jolly giant labours told of peace obtained, and there could be no peace without his prize.

He listened to the workmen's foot-falls. The solitary sound and steady motion of their feet were eloquent of early morning in a city, not less than the changes of light in heaven above the roofs. With the golden light came numbers, workmen still. Their tread on the stones roused some of his working thoughts, like an old tune in his head, and he watched the scattered files passing on, disciplined by their daily necessities, easily manageable if their necessities are but justly considered. These numbers are the brute force of earth, which must have the earth in time, as they had it in the dawn of our world, and then they entered into bondage for not knowing how to use it. They will have it again: they have it partially, at times, in the despot, who is only the reflex of their brute force, and can give them only a shadow of their claim. They will have it all, when they have illumination to see and trust to the leadership of a greater force than they— in force of brain, in the spiritual force of ideas; ideas founded on justice;

and not the justice of these days of the governing few whose wits are bent to steady our column of civilized humanity by a combination of props and jugglers' arts, but a justice coming of the recognized needs of majorities, which will base the column on a broad plinth for safety — broad as the base of yonder mountain's towering white immensity — and will be the guarantee for the solid uplifting of our civilization at last. "Right, thou!" he apostrophized the old Ironer, at a point of his meditation. "And right, thou! more largely right!" he thought, further advanced in it, of the great Giuseppe, the Genoese. "And right am I too, between that metal-rail of a politician and the deep dreamer, each of them incomplete for want of an element of the other!" Practically and in vision right was Alvan, for those two opposites met fusing in him: like the former, he counted on the supremacy of might; like the latter, he distinguished where it lay in perpetuity.

During his younger years he had been like neither in the moral curb they could put on themselves — particularly the southern-blooded man. He had resembled the naturally impatient northerner most, though not so supple for business as he. But now he possessed the calmness of the Genoese; he had strong self-command now; he had the principle that life is too short for the indulgence of public fretfulness or of private quarrels; too valuable for fruitless risks; too sacred, one may say, for the shedding of blood on personal grounds. Oh! he had himself well under, fear not. He could give and take from opposition. And rightly so, seeing that he confessed to his own bent for sarcastically stinging: he was therefore bound to endure a retort. Speech for speech, pamphlet for pamphlet, he could be temperate. Nay, he defied an adversary to produce in him the sensation of intemperateness; so there would not be much danger of his being excited to betray it. Shadowily he thought of the hard words hurled at him by the Rüdigers, and of the injury Clotilde's father did him by plotting to rob him of his daughter. But how had an Alvan replied? — with the arts of peaceful fence victoriously. He conceived of no temptation to his repressed irascibility save the political. A day might come for him and the vehement old Ironer to try their mettle in a tussle.

On that day he would have to be wary, but, as Alvan felt assured, he would be more master of himself than his antagonist. He was for the young world, in the brain of a new order of things; the other based his unbending system on the visions of a feudal chief, and would win a great step perchance, but there he would stop: he was not with the future!

This immediate prospect of a return to serenity after his recent charioteering, had set him thinking of himself and his days to come, which hung before him in a golden haze that was tranquillizing. He had a name, he had a station: he wanted power and he saw it approaching.

He wanted a wife too. Colonel von Tresten took coffee with him previous to the start with Dr. Störchel to General von Rüdiger's house. Alvan consequently was unable any longer to think of a wife in the abstract. He wanted Clotilde. Here was a man going straight to her, going to see her, positively to see her and hear her voice! — almost instantly to hear her voice, and see her eyes and hair, touch her hand. Oh! and rally her, rouse her wit; and be able to tell him the flower she wore for the day, and where she wore it — at her temples, or sliding to the back hair, or in her bosom, or at her waist! She had innumerable tricks of indication in these shifty pretty ways of hers, and was full of varying speech to the cunning reader of her.

"But keep her to seriousness," Alvan said. "Our meeting must be early to-day — early in the afternoon. She is not unlikely to pretend to trifle. She has not seen me for some time, and will probably enough play at emancipation and speak of the 'singular impatience of the seigneur Alvan.' Don't you hear her? I swear to those very words! She 'loves her liberty,' and she curves her fan and taps her foot. 'The seigneur Alvan appears pressed for time.' She has 'letters to write to friends to-day.' Stop that! I can't join in play: to-morrow, if she likes; not to-day. Or not till I have her by the hand. She shall be elf and fairy, French coquette, whatever she pleases to-morrow, and I'll be satisfied. All I beg is for plain dealing on a business matter. This is a business matter, a business meeting. I thoroughly know the girl's heart, and know that in winning the interview I win her. Only" — he pressed his friend's arm — "but, my dear Tresten, you understand. You're a luckier fellow than I — for the time, at all events. Make it as short as you can. You'll find me here. I shall take a book — one of the Pandects. I don't suppose I shall work. I feel idle. Any book handy; anything will interest me. I should walk or row on the lake, but I would rather be sure of readiness for your return. You meet Störchel at the General's house?"

"The appointment was at the house," Tresten said.

"I have not seen him this morning. I know of nothing to prepare him for. You see, it was invariable with her: as soon as she met me she had twice her spirit: and that she knows; — she was a new woman, ten times the happier for having some grains of my courage. So she'll be glad to come to terms and have me by to support her. Press it, if necessary; otherwise she might be disappointed, my dear fellow. Störchel looks on, and observes, and that's about all he can do, or need do. Up Mont Blanc to-day, Tresten! It's the very day for an ascent: — one of the rare crystalline jewels coming in a Swiss August; we should see the kingdoms of the earth — and a Republic! But I could climb with all my heart in a snowstorm to-day. Andes on Himalayas! as high as you like. The Republic by the way, small enough in the ring of empires and monarchies, if you measure it geometrically! You remember the laugh at the exact elevation of Mount Olympus? But Zeus's eagle sat on it, and top me Olympus, after you have imagined the eagle aloft there! after Homer, is the meaning. That will be one of the lessons for our young Republicans — to teach them not to give themselves up to the embrace of dead materialism because, as they fancy, they have had to depend on material weapons for carving their way, and have had no help from other quarters. A suicidal delusion! The spiritual weapon has done most, and always does. They are sons of an idea. They deny their parentage when they scoff at idealism. It's a tendency we shall have to guard against; it leads back to the old order of things, if we do not trim our light. — She is waiting for you! Go. You will find me here. And don't forget my instructions. Appoint for the afternoon — not late. Too near night will seem like Orpheus going below, and I hope to meet a living woman, not a ghost — ha! coloured like a lantern in a cavern, good Lord! Covered with lichen! Say three o'clock, not later. The reason is, I want to have it over early and be sure of what I am doing; I'm bothered by it; I shall have to make arrangements . . . a thousand little matters . . . telegraph to Paris, I daresay; she's fond of Paris, and I must learn who's there to meet her. Now start. I'll walk a dozen steps with you. I think of her as if, since we parted, she had been sitting on a throne in Erebus, and must be ghastly. I had a dream of a dead tree that upset me. In fact, you see I must have it over. The whole affair makes me feel too young."

Tresten advised him to spend an hour with the baroness.

"I can't; she makes me feel too old," said Alvan. "She talks. She listens, but I don't want to speak. Dead silence! — let it be a dash of the pen till you return. As for these good people hurrying to their traffic, and tourists and loungers, they have a trick for killing time without hurting him. I wish I had. I try to smother a minute, and up the old fellow jumps quivering all over and threatening me body and soul. They don't appear as if they had news on their faces this morning. I've not seen a newspaper and won't look at one. Here we separate. Be formal in mentioning me to her but be particularly civil. I know you have the right tone: she's a critical puss. Days like these are the days for her to be out. There goes a parasol like one I've seen her carry. Stay — no! Don't forget my instructions. Paris for a time. It may be the Pyrenees. Paris on our way back. She would like the Pyrenees. It's not too late for society at Luchon and Cauterets. She likes mountains, she mounts well: in any case, plenty of mules can be had. Paris to wind up with. Paris will be fuller about the beginning of October."

He had quitted Tresten, and was talking to himself, cheating himself, not discordantly at all. The poet of the company within him claimed the word and was allowed by the others to dilate on Clotilde's likings, and the honeymoon or post — honeymoon amusements to be provided for her in Pyrenean valleys, and Parisian theatres and salons. She was friande of chocolates, bon-bons: she enjoyed fine pastry, had a real relish of good wine. She should have the best of everything; he knew the spots of the very best that Paris could supply, in confiseurs and restaurants, and in millinery likewise. A lively recollection of the prattle of Parisian ladies furnished names and addresses likely to prove invaluable to Clotilde. He knew actors and actresses, and managers of theatres, and mighty men in letters. She should have the cream of Paris. Does she hint at rewarding him for his trouble? The thought of her indebted lips, half closed, asking him how to repay him, sprang his heart to his throat.

## CHAPTER XVI.

THEN he found himself saying: "At the age I touch!"...

At the age of forty, men that love love rootedly. If the love is plucked from them, the life goes with it.

He backed on his physical pride, a stout bulwark. His forty years — the forty, the fifty, the sixty of Alvan, matched the twenties and thirties of other men.

Still it was true that he had reached an age when the desire to plant his affections in a dear fair bosom fixedly was natural. Fairer, dearer than she was never one on earth! He stood bareheaded for coolness, looking in the direction Tresten had taken, his forehead shining and eyes charged with the electrical activity of the mind, reading intensely all who passed him, without a thought upon any of these objects in their passage. The people were read, penetrated, and flung off as from a whirring of wheels; to cut their place in memory sharp as in steel when imagination shall by and by renew the throbbing of that hour, if the wheels be not stilled. The world created by the furnaces of vitality inside him absorbed his mind; and strangely, while receiving multitudinous vivid impressions, he did not commune with one, was unaware of them. His thick black hair waved and glistened over the fine aquiline of his face. His throat was open to the breeze. His great breast and head were joined by a massive column of throat that gave volume for the coursing of the blood to fire the battery of thought, perchance in a tempest overflood it, extinguish it. His fortieth year was written on his complexion and presence: it was the fortieth of a giant growth that will bend at the past eightieth as little as the rock-pine, should there come no uprooting tempest. It said manhood, and breathed of settled strength of muscle, nerve, and brain.

Of the people passing, many knew him not, but marked him; some knew him by repute, one or two his person. To all of them he was a noticeable figure; even those of sheeplike nature, having an inclination to start upon the second impulse in the flanks of curious sheep when their first has been arrested by the appearance of one not of their kind, acknowledged the eminence of his bearing. There may have been a passenger in the street who could tell the double tale of the stick he swung in his hand, showing a gleam of metal, whereon were engraved names of the lurid historic original owner, and of the donor and the recipient. According to the political sentiments of the narrator would his tale be coloured, and a simple walking-stick would be clothed in Tarquin guilt for striking off heads of the upper ranks of Frenchmen till the blood of them topped the handle, or else wear hues of wonder, seem very memorable, fit at least for a museum. If the Christian aristocrat might shrink from it in terror and loathing, the Paynim Republican of deep dye would be ready to kiss it with veneration. But, assuming them to have a certain bond of manliness, both agree in pronouncing the deed a right valiant and worthy one, which caused this instrument to be presented to Alvan by a famous doctor, who, hearing of his repudiation of the duel, and of his gallant and triumphant defence of himself against a troop of ruffians, enemies or scum of their city, at night, by the aid of a common stout pedestrian stick, alone in a dark alley of the public park, sent him, duly mounted and engraved, an illustrious fellow to the weapon of defence, as a mode of commemorating his just abhorrence of bloodshed and his peaceful bravery.

Observers of him would probably speculate on his features and the carriage of his person as he went by them; with a result in their minds that can be of no import to us, men's general speculations being directed by their individual aims and their moods, their timidities, prejudices, envies, rivalries; but none could contest that he was a potential figure. If to know him the rising demagogue of the time dressed him in such terrors as to make him appear an impending Attila of the voracious hordes which live from hand to mouth, without intervention of a banker and property to cry truce to the wolf, he would have shone under a different aspect enough to send them to the poets to solve their perplexity, had the knowledge been subjoined that this terrific devastator swinging the sanguinary stick was a slave of love, who staked his all upon his love, loved up to his capacity desperately, loved a girl, and hung upon her voice to hear whether his painful knocking at a door should gain him admittance to the ranks of the orderly citizens of the legitimately-satiated passions, or else — the voice of a girl annihilate him.

He loved like the desert-bred Eastern, as though his blood had never ceased to be steeped in its fountain Orient; loved barbarously, but with a compelling resolve to control his blood and act and be the civilized man, sober by virtue of his lady's gracious aid. In fact, it was the civilized man in him that had originally sought the introduction to her, with a bribe to the untameable. The former had once led, and hoped to lead again. Alvan was a revolutionist in imagination, the workman's friend in rational sympathy, their leader upon mathematical calculation, but a lawyer, a reasoner in law, and therefore of necessity a cousin germane, leaning to become an ally, of the Philistines — the founders and main supporters of his book of the Law. And so, between the nature of his blood, and the inclination of his mind, Alvan set his heart on a damsel of the Philistines, endowed with their trained elegancies and governed by some of their precepts, but suitable to his wildness in her reputation for originality, suiting him in her cultivated liveliness and her turn for luxury. Only the Philistines breed these choice beauties, put forth these delicate fresh young buds of girls; and only here and there among them is there an exquisite, eccentric, yet passably decorous Clotilde. What his brother politicians never discovered in him, and the baroness partly suspected, through her interpretation of things opposing her sentiments, Clotilde uncloaks. Catching and mastering her, his wilder animation may be appeased, but his political life is threatened with a diversion of its current, for he will be uxorious, impassioned to gratify the tastes and whims of a youthful wife; the Republican will be in danger of playing prematurely for power to seat her beside him high: while at the same time, children, perchance, and his hardening lawyer's head are secretly Philistinizing the demagogue, blunting the fine edge of his Radicalism, turning him into a slow-stepping Liberal, otherwise your half-Conservative in his convictions. Can she think it much to have married that drab-coloured unit? Power must be grasped. . . .

His watch told him that Tresten was now beholding her, or just about to. The stillness of the heavens was remarkable. The hour held breath. She delayed her descent from her chamber. He saw how she touched at her hair, more distinctly than he saw the lake before his eyes. He watched her, and the growl of a coming roar from him rebuked her tricky deliberateness. Deciding at last, she slips down the stairs like a waterfall, and is in the room, erect, composed — if you do not lay ear against her bosom. Tresten stares at her, owns she is worth a struggle. Love does this, friend Tresten! Love, that stamps out prejudice and bids inequality be smooth. Tresten stares and owns she is worth heavier labours, worse than his friend has endured. Love does it! Love, that hallows a stranger's claim to the flower of a proud garden: Love has won her the freedom to suffer herself to be chosen by the stranger. What matters which of them toiled to bring them to so sweet an end! It was not either of them, but Love. By and by, after acting serenest innocent, suddenly broken, she will be copious of sad confessions. That will be in their secrecy: in the close and boundless together of clasped hands. Deep eyes, that give him in realms of light within light all that he has dreamed of rapturousness and blessedness, you are threatened with a blinding kiss if you look abashed: — if her voice shall dare repeat another of those foolish self-reproaches, it shall be construed as a petition for further kisses. Silence! he said to her, imagining that he had been silent, and enjoying silence with a perfect quietude beyond the trouble of a thought of her kisses and his happiness. His full heart craved for the infinity of silence.

Another moment, and he was counting to her the days, hours, minutes, which had been the gulf of torture between then and now — the separation and the reunion: he was voluble, living to speak, and a pause was only for the drawing of most blissful breath.

His watch went slowly. She was beginning to drop her eyelids in front of Tresten. Oh! he knew her so well. He guessed the length of her acting, and the time for her earnestness. She would have to act a coquette at first to give herself a countenance; and who would not pardon the girl for putting on a mask? who would fail to see the mask? But he knew her so well: she would not trifle very long: his life on it, that she will soon falter! her bosom will lift, lift and check: a word from Tresten then, if he is a friend, and she melts to the truth in her. Alvan heard her saying: "I will see him: yes, to-day. Let him appoint. He may come when he likes — come at once."

"My life on it!" he swore by his unerring knowledge of her, the certainty that she loved him.

He had walked into a quarter of the town strange to him, he thought; he had no recollection of the look of the street. A friend came up and put him in the right way, walking back with him. This was General Leczel, a famous leader of one of the heroical risings whose passage through blood and despair have led to the broader law men ask for when they name freedom devotedly. Alvan stated the position of his case to Leczel with continental frankness regarding a natural theme, and then pursued the talk on public affairs, to the note of: "What but knocks will ever open the Black-Yellow Head to the fact that we are no longer in the first years of the eighteenth century!"

Leczel left him at his hotel steps, promising to call on him before night. Tresten had not returned, neither he nor the advocate, and he had been absent fully an hour. He was not in sight right or left. Alvan went to his room, looked at his watch, and out of the window, incapable of imagining any event. He began to breathe as if an atmosphere thick as water were pressing round him. Unconsciously he had staked his all on the revelation the moment was to bring. So little a thing! His intellect weighed the littleness of it, but he had become level with it; he magnified it with the greatness of his desire, and such was his nature that the great desire of a thing withheld from him and his own, as he could think, made the world a whirlpool till he had it. He waited, figureable by nothing so much as a wild horse in captivity sniffing the breeze, when the flanks of the quivering beast are like a wind-struck barley-field, and his nerves are cords, and his nostrils trumpet him: he is flame kept under and straining to rise.

## CHAPTER XVII.

THE baroness expected to see Alvan in the morning, for he kept appointments, and he had said he would come. She conceived that she was independent of personal wishes on the subject of Clotilde; the fury of his passion prohibited her forming any of the wishes we send up to destiny when matters interesting us are in suspense, whether we have liberated minds or not. She thought the girl would grant the interview; was sure the creature would yield in his presence; and then there was an end to the shining of Alvan! Supposing the other possibility, he had shown her such fierce illuminations of eye and speech that she foresaw it would be a blazing of the insurrectionary beacon-fires of hell with him. He was a man of angels and devils. The former had long been conquering, but the latter were far from extinct. His passion for this shallow girl had consigned him to the lower host. Let him be thwarted, his desperation would be unlikely to stop at legal barriers. His lawyer's head would be up and armed astoundingly to oppose the law; he would read, argue, and act with hot conviction upon the reverse of every text of law. She beheld him storming the father's house to have out Clotilde, reluctant or conniving; and he harangued the people, he bore off his captive, he held her firmly as he had sworn he would; he defied authority, he was a public rebel — he with his detected little secret aim, which he nursed like a shamed mother of an infant, fond but afraid to be proud of it! She had seen that he aimed at standing well with the world and being one with it honourably: holding to his principles of course: but a disposition that way had been perceived, and the vision of him in open rebellion because of his shy catching at the thread of an alliance with the decorous world, carved an ironic line on her jaw.

Full surely he would not be baffled without smiting the world on the face. And he might suffer for it; the Rüdigers would suffer likewise.

She considered them very foolish people. Her survey of the little nobility beneath her station had previously enabled her to account for their disgust of such a suitor as Alvan, and maintain that they would oppose him tooth and nail. Owing to his recent success, the anticipation of a peaceful surrender to him seemed now on the whole to carry most weight. This girl gives Alvan her hand and her family repudiate her. Volatile, flippant, shallow as she is, she must have had some turn for him; a physical spell was on her once, and it will be renewed when they meet. It sometimes inspires a semblance of courage; she may determine; she may be steadfast long enough for him to take his measures to bear her away. And the Brocken witches congratulate him on his prize!

Almost better would it be, she thought, that circumstance should thwart him and kindle his own demon element.

The forenoon, the noon, the afternoon, went round.

Late in the evening her door was flung wide for Colonel von Tresten.

She looked her interrogative "Well?" His features were not used to betray the course of events.

"How has it gone?" she said.

He replied: "As I told you. I fancied I gauged the hussy pretty closely."

"She will not see him?"

"Not she."

The baroness crossed her arms.

"And Alvan?"

The colonel shrugged. It was not done to tease a tremulous woman, for she was calm. It painted the necessary consequence of the refusal: an explosion of Ætna, and she saw it.

"Where is he now?" said she.

"At his hotel."

"Alone?"

"Leczel is with him."

"That looks like war."

Tresten shrugged again. "It might have been foreseen by everybody concerned in the affair. The girl does not care for him one corner of an eye! She stood up before us cool as at a dancing-lesson, swore she had never committed herself to an oath to him, sneered at him. She positively sneered. Her manner to me assures me without question that if he had stood in my place she would have insulted him."

"Scarcely. She would do in his absence what she would not do under his eyes," remarked the baroness. "It's decided, then?"

"Quite."

"Will he be here to-night?"

"I think not."

"Was she really insolent?"

"For a girl in her position, she was."

"Did you repeat her words to him?"

"Some of them."

"What description of insolence?"

"She spoke of his vanity. . . ."

"Proceed."

"It was more her manner to me, as the one of the two appearing as his friend. She was tolerably civil to Störchel: and the difference of behaviour must have been designed, for she not only looked at Störchel in a way to mark the difference, she addressed him rather eagerly before we turned on our heels, to tell him she would write to *him*, and let him have her reply in a letter. He will get some coquettish rigmarole."

"That seems monstrous!—if one could be astonished by her," said the baroness. "When is she to write?"

"She may write: the letter will find no receiver," said Tresten, significantly raising his eyebrows. "The legal gentleman is gone—blown from a gun! He's off home.

He informed me that he should write to the General, throwing up his office, and an end to his share in the business."

"There was no rudeness to the poor man?"

"Dear me, no. But imagine a quiet little advocate, very precise and silky — you've had a hint of him — and all of a sudden the client he has by the ear swells into a tremendous beast — a combination of lion and elephant — bellows and shakes the room, stops and stamps before him, discharging an unintelligible flood of racy vernacular punctuated in thunder. You hear him and see him! Alvan lost his head — some of his hair too. The girl is not worth a lock. But he's past reason."

"He takes it so," said the baroness, musing. "It will be the sooner over. She never cared for him a jot. And there's the sting. He has called up the whole world in an amphitheatre to see a girl laugh him to scorn. Hard for any man to bear! — Alvan of all men! Why does he not come here? He might rage at me for a day and a night, and I would rock him to sleep in the end. However, he has *done* nothing?"

That was the point. The baroness perceived it to be a serious point, and repeated the question sharply. "Has he been to the house? — no? — writing?"

Tresten dropped a nod.

"Not to the girl, I suppose. To the father?" said she.

"He has written to the General."

"You should have stopped it."

"Tell a vedette to stop cavalry. You're not thinking of the man. He's in a white frenzy."

"I will go to him."

"You will do wrong. Leave him to spout the stuff and get rid of his poison. I remember a sister of poor Nuciotti's going to him after he had let his men walk into a trap — and that was through a woman: and he was quieted, and the chief overlooked it; and two days after, Nuciotti blew his brains out. He'd have been alive now if he had been left alone. Furious cursing is a natural relief to some men, like women's weeping. He has written a savage letter to her father, sending the girl to the deuce with the name she deserves, and challenging the General."

"That letter is despatched?"

"Rüdiger has it by this time."

The baroness fixed her eyes on Tresten: she struck her lap. "Alvan! Is it he? But the General is old, gouty, out of the lists. There can be no fighting. He apologized to you for his daughter's insolence to me. He will not fight, be sure."

"Perhaps not," Tresten said.

"As for the girl, Alvan has the fullest right to revile her: it cannot be too widely known. I could cry: 'What wisdom there is in men when they are mad!' We must allow it to counterbalance breaches of ordinary courtesy. *With the name she deserves,*' you say? He pitched the very name at her character plainly? — called her what she is?"

The baroness could have borne to hear it: she had no feminine horror of the staining epithet for that sex. But a sense of the distinction between camps and courts restrained the soldier. He spoke of a discharge of cuttle-fish ink at the character of the girl, and added: "The bath's a black one for her, and they had better keep it private. Regrettable, no doubt, but it's probably true, and he's out of his mind. It would be dangerous to check him: he'd force his best friend to fight. Leczel is with him and gives him head. It's about time for me to go back to him, for there may be business."

The baroness thought it improbable. She was hoping that with Alvan's eruption the drop-scene would fall.

Tresten spoke of the possibility. He knew the contents of the letter, and knew further that a copy of it, with none of the pregnant syllables expunged, had been forwarded to Prince Marko. He counselled calm waiting for a certain number of hours. The baroness committed herself to a promise to wait. Now that Alvan had broken off from the baleful girl, the worst must have been passed, she thought.

He had broken with the girl: she reviewed him under the light of that sole fact. So the edge of the cloud obscuring him was lifted, and he would again be the man she prized and hoped much of! How thickly he had been obscured was visible to her through a retreating sensation of scorn of him for his mad excesses, which she had not known herself to entertain while he was writhing in the toils, and very bluntly and dismissingly felt now that his madness was at its climax. An outrageous lunatic fit, that promised to release him from his fatal passion, seemed, on the contrary, respectable in essence if not in the display. Wives he should have by fifties and hundreds if he wanted them, she thought in her great-heartedness, reflecting on the one whose threatened pretensions to be his mate were slain by the title flung at her, and merited. The word (she could guess it) was an impassable gulf, a wound beyond healing. It pronounced in a single breath the girl's right name and his pledge of a return to sanity. For it was the insanest he could do; it uttered anathema on his love of her; it painted his white glow of unreason and fierce ire at the scorn which her behaviour flung upon every part of his character that was tenderest with him. After speaking such things a man comes to his senses or he dies. So thought the baroness, and she was not more than commonly curious to hear how the Rüdigers had taken the insult they had brought on themselves, and not unwilling to wait to see Alvan till he was cool. His vanity, when threatening to bleed to the death, would not be civil to the surgeon before the second or third dressing of his wound.

## CHAPTER XVIII.

In the house of the Rüdigers there was commotion. Clotilde sat apart from it, locked in her chamber. She had performed her crowning act of obedience to her father by declining the interview with Alvan, and as a consequence she was full of grovelling revolt.

Two things had helped her to carry out her engagement to submit in this final instance of dutifulness: one was the sight of that hateful rigid face and glacier eye of Tresten; the other was the loophole she left for subsequent insurgency by engaging to write to Count Hollinger's envoy, Dr. Störchel. She had gazed most earnestly at him, that he might not mistake her meaning, and the little man's pair of spectacles had, she fancied, been dim. He was touched.

Here was a friend! Here was the friend she required, the external aid, the fresh evasion, the link with Alvan! Now to write to him to bind him to his beautiful human emotion. By contrast with the treacherous Tresten, whose iciness roused her to defiance, the nervous little advocate seemed an emissary of the skies, and she invoked her treasure-stores of the craven's craftiness in revolt to compose a letter that should move him, melt the good angel to espouse her cause. He was to be taught to understand — nay, angelically he would understand at once — why she had behaved apparently so contradictorily. Fettered, cruelly constrained by threats and wily sermons upon her duty to her family, terrorized, a prisoner 'beside this blue lake, in sight of the sublimest scenery of earth,' and hating his associate — hating him, she repeated and underscored — she had belied herself; she was willing to meet Alvan, she wished to meet him. She could open her heart to Alvan's true friend — his only true friend. He would instantly discern her unhappy plight. In the presence of his associate she could explain nothing, do nothing but what she had done. He had *frozen* her. She had good reason to know that man for her enemy. She could prove him a traitor to Alvan. Certain though she was from the first moment of Dr. Störchel's integrity and kindness of heart, she had stood petrified before him, as if affected by some wicked spell. She owned she had utterly belied herself; she protested she had been no free agent.

The future labours in her cause were thrown upon Dr. Störchel's shoulders, but with such compliments to him on his mission from above as emissary angels are presumed to be sensibly affected by.

The letter was long, involved, rather eloquent when she forgot herself and wrote herself, and intentionally very feminine, after the manner of supplicatory ladies appealing to lawyers, whom they would sway by the feeble artlessness of a sex that must confide in their possession of a heart, their heads being too awful.

She was directing the letter when Marko Romaris gave his name outside her door. He was her intimate, her trustiest ally; he was aware of her design to communicate with Dr. Störchel, and came to tell her it would be a waste of labour. He stood there singularly pale and grave, unlike the sprightly slave she petted on her search for a tyrant. "Too late," he said, pointing to the letter she held. "Dr. Störchel has gone."

She could not believe it, for Störchel had informed her that he would remain three days. Her powers of belief were more heavily taxed when Marko said: "Alvan has challenged your father to fight him." With that he turned on his heel; he had to assist in the deliberations of the family.

She clasped her temples. The collision of ideas driven together by Alvan and a duel — Alvan challenging her father — Alvan, the contemner of the senseless appeal to arms for the settlement of personal disputes! — darkened her mind. She ran about the house plying all whom she met for news and explanations; but her young brother was absent, her sisters were ignorant, and her parents were closeted in consultation with the gentlemen. At night Marko sent her word that she might sleep in peace, for things would soon be arranged and her father had left the city.

She went to her solitude to study the hard riddle of her shattered imagination of Alvan. The fragments would not suffer joining, they assailed her in huge heaps; and she did not ask herself whether she had ever known him, but what disruption it was that had unsettled the reason of the strongest man alive. At times he came flashing through the scud of her thoughts magnificently in person, and how to stamp that splendid figure of manhood on a madman's conduct was the task she supposed herself to be attempting while she shrank from it, and worshipped the figure, abhorred the deed. She could not unite them. He was like some great cathedral organ foully handled in the night by demons. He, whose lucent reason was an unclouded sky over every complexity of our sphere, he to crave to fight! to seek the life-blood of the father of his beloved! More unintelligible than this was it to reflect that he must know the challenge to be of itself a bar to his meeting his Clotilde ever again. She led her senses round to weep, and produced a state of mental drowning for a truce to the bitter riddle.

Quiet reigned in the household next day, and for the

length of the day. Her father had departed, her mother treated her vixenishly, snubbing her for a word, but the ugly business of yesterday seemed a matter settled and dismissed. Alvan, then, had been appeased. He was not a man of blood: he was the humanest of men. She was able to reconstruct him under the beams of his handsome features and his kingly smile. She could occasionally conjure them up in their vividness; but had she not in truth been silly to yield to spite and send him back the photographs of him with his presents, so that he should have the uttermost remnant of the gifts he asked for? Had he really asked to have anything back? She inclined to doubt all that had been done and said since their separation — if only it were granted her to look on a photograph showing him as he was actually before their misunderstanding! The sun-tracing would not deceive, as her own tricks of imageing might do: seeing him as he was then, the hour would be revived, she would certainly feel him as he lived and breathed now. Thus she fancied, on the effort to get him to her heart after the shock he had dealt it, for he had become almost a stranger, as a god that has taken human shape and character.

Next to the sight of Alvan her friend Marko was welcome. The youth visited her in the evening, and with a glitter of his large black eyes bent to her, and began talking incomprehensibly of leave-taking and farewell, until she cried aloud that she had riddles enough: one was too much. What had he to say? She gave him her hand to encourage him. She listened, and soon it was her hand that mastered his in the grasp, though she was putting questions incredulously, with an understanding duller than her instinct. Or how if the frightful instinct while she listened shot lightnings in her head, whose revelations were too intelligible to be looked at? We think it devilish when our old nature is incandescent to talk to us in this way, kindled by its vilest in hoping, hungering, and fearing; and we call on the civilized mind to disown it. The tightened grasp of her hand confessed her understanding of the thing she pressed to hear repeated, for the sake of seeming to herself to repudiate it under an accumulating horror, at the same time that the repetition doubly and trebly confirmed it, so as to exon-

erate her criminal sensations by casting the whole burden
on the material fact.

Marko, with her father's consent and the approval of the
friends of the family, had taken up Alvan's challenge!
That was the tale. She saw him dead in the act of
telling it.

"What?" she cried: "what?" and then: "You?"
and her fingers were bonier in their clutch: "Let me hear.
It can't be!" She snapped at herself for not pitying him
more, but a sword had flashed to cut her gordian knot:
she saw him dead, the obstacle removed, the man whom
her parents opposed to Alvan swept away: she saw him as
a black gate breaking to a flood of light. She had never
invoked it, never wished, never dreamed it, but if it was to
be? . . . "Oh! impossible. One of us is crazy. You to
fight? . . . they put it upon you? You fight *him*? But
it is cruel, it is abominable. Incredible! You have accepted the challenge, you say?"

He answered that he had, and gazed into her eyes for
love.

She blinked over them, crying out against parents and
friends for their heartlessness in permitting him to fight.

"This is positive? This is really true?" she said,
burning and dreading to realize the magical change it
pointed on, and touching him with her other hand, loathing herself, loathing parents and friends who had brought
her to the plight of desiring some terrible event in sheer
necessity. Not she, it was the situation they had created
which was guilty! By dint of calling out on their heartlessness, and a spur of conscience, she roused the feeling
of compassion:

"But, Marko! Marko! poor child! you cannot fight;
you have never fired a pistol or a gun in your life. Your
health was always too delicate for these habits of men;
and you could not pull a trigger taking aim, do you not
know?"

"I have been practising for a couple of hours to-day,"
he said.

Compassion thrilled her. "A couple of hours! Unhappy
boy! But do you not know that he is a dead shot? He
is famous for his aim. He never misses. He can do all

the duellist's wonders both with sword and pistol, and that is why he was respected when he refused the duel because he — before these parents of mine drove him . . . and me! I think we are both mad — he despised duelling. He! He! Alvan! who has challenged my father! I have heard him speak of duelling as cowardly. But what is he? what has he changed to? And it would be cowardly to kill you, Marko."

"I take my chance," Marko said.

"You have no chance. His aim is unerring." She insisted on the deadliness of his aim, and dwelt on it with a gloating delight that her conscience approved, for she was persuading the youth to shun his fatal aim. "If you stood against him he would not spare you — perhaps not; I fear he would not, as far as I know him now. He can be terrible in wrath. I think he would warn you; but two men face to face! and he suspecting that you cross his path! Find some way of avoiding him. Do, I entreat you. By your love of me! Oh! no blood. I do not want to lose you. I could not bear it."

"Would you regret me?" said he.

Her eyes fell on his, and the beauty of those great dark eyes made her fondness for him legible. He caused her a spasm of anguish, foreknowing him doomed. She thought that haply this devoted heart was predestined to be the sacrifice which should bring her round to Alvan. She murmured phrases of dissuasion until her hollow voice broke; she wept for being speechless, and turned upon Providence and her parents, in railing at whom a voice of no ominous empty sound was given her; and still she felt more warmly than railing expressed, only her voice shrank back from a tone of feeling. She consoled herself with the reflection that utterance was inadequate. Besides, her active good sense echoed Marko ringingly when he cited the usages of their world and the impossibility of his withdrawing or wishing to withdraw from the line of a challenge accepted. It was destiny. She bowed her head lower and lower, oppressed without and within, unwilling to look at him. She did not look when he left her.

The silence of him encouraged her head to rise. She stared about: his phantom seemed present, and for a time she beheld him both upright in life and stretched in death. It could not be her fault that he should die! it was the fatality. How strange it was! Providence, after bitterly misusing her, offered this reparation through the death of Marko.

Possibly she ought to run out and beseech Alvan to spare the innocent youth. She stood up trembling on her legs. She called to Alvan. "Do not put blood between us. Oh! I love you more than ever. Why did you let that horrible man you take for a friend come here? I hate him, and cannot feel my love of you when I see him. He chills me to the bone. He made me say the reverse of what was in my heart. But spare poor Marko! You have no cause for jealousy. You would be above it, if you had. Do not aim; fire in the air. Do not let me kiss that hand and think . . ."

She sank to her chair, exclaiming: "I am a prisoner!" She could not walk two steps; she was imprisoned by the interdict of the house and the paralysis of her limbs. Providence decreed that she must abide the result. Dread Power! To be dragged to her happiness through a river of blood was indeed dreadful, but the devotional sense of reliance upon hidden wisdom in the direction of human affairs when it appears considerate of our wishes, inspirited her to be ready for what Providence was about to do, mysterious in its beneficence that it was! It is the dark goddess Fortune to the craven. The craven with desires will offer up bloody sacrifices to it submissively. The craven, with desires expecting to be blest, is a zealot of the faith which ascribes the direction of events to the outer world. Her soul was in full song to that contriving agency, and she with the paralyzed limbs became practically active, darting here and there over the room, burning letters, packing a portable bundle of clothes, in preparation for the domestic confusion of the morrow when the body of Marko would be driven to their door, and amid the wailing and the hubbub she would escape unnoticed to Alvan, Providence-guided! Out of the house would then signify assuredly to Alvan's arms.

The prospect might have seemed too heavenly to be realizable had she not been sensible of paying heavily for it; and thus, as he would wish to be, was Marko of double service to her; for she was truly fond of the beautiful and chivalrous youth, and far from wishing to lose him. His blood was on the heads of those who permitted him to face the danger! She would have felt for him still more tenderly if it were permitted to a woman's heart to enfold two men at a time. This, it would seem, she cannot do: she is compelled by the painful restriction sadly to consent that one of them should be swept away.

Night passed dragging and galloping. In the very early light she thought of adding some ornaments to her bundle of necessaries. She learnt of the object of her present faith to be provident on her own behalf, and dressed in two of certain garments which would have swoln her bundle too much.

This was the day of Providence: she had strung herself to do her part in it and gone through the pathos of her fatalism above stairs in her bedroom before Marko took his final farewell of her, so she could speak her " Heaven be with you!" unshaken, though sadly. Her father had returned. To be away from him, and close to her bundle, she hurried to her chamber and awaited the catastrophe, like one expecting to be raised from the vaults. Carriage wheels would give her the first intimation of it. Slow, very slow, would imply badly wounded, she thought: dead, if the carriage stopped some steps from the house and one of the seconds of the poor boy descended to make the melancholy announcement. She could not but apprehend the remorselessness of the decree. Death, it would probably be! Alvan had resolved to sweep him off the earth. She could not blame Alvan for his desperate passion, though pitying the victim of it. In any case the instant of the arrival of the carriage was her opportunity marked by the finger of Providence rendered visible, and she sat rocking her parcel on her lap. Her love of Alvan now was mixed with an alluring terror of him as an immediate death-dealer who stood against red-streaked heavens, more grandly satanic in his angry mightiness than she had ever realized that figure, and she trembled and shuddered, fearing to meet him, yearning to be taken to him, to close her eyes on his breast in blindest happiness. She gave the very sob for the occasion

A carriage drove at full speed to the door. Full speed could not be the pace for a funeral load. That was a visitor to her father on business. She waited for fresh wheels, telling herself she would be patient and must be ready.

Her pathos was ready and scarcely controllable. The tear thickened on her eyelid as she projected her mind on the grief she would soon be undergoing for Marko: or at least she would undergo it subsequently; she would certainly mourn for him. She dared not proceed to an accumulated enumeration of his merits, as her knowledge of the secret of pathos knew to be most moving, in an extreme fear that she might weaken her required energies for action at the approaching signal.

Feet came rushing up the stairs: her door was thrown open, and the living Marko, stranger than a dead, stood present. He had in his look an expectation that she would be glad to behold him, and he asked her, and she said: "Oh, yes, she was glad, of course." She was glad that Alvan had pardoned him for his rashness; she was vexed that her projected confusion of the household had been thwarted: vexed, petrified with astonishment.

"But how if I tell you that Alvan is wounded?" he almost wept to say.

Clotilde informs the world that she laughed on hearing this. She was unaware of her ground for laughing. It was the laugh of the tragic comedian.

Could one believe in a Providence capable of letting such a sapling and weakling strike down the most magnificent stature upon earth?

"*You — him?*" she said, in the tremendous compression of her contempt.

She laughed. The world is upside down — a world without light, or pointing finger, or affection for special favourites, and therefore bereft of all mysterious and attractive wisdom, a crazy world, a corpse of a world — if this be true!

But it can still be disbelieved.

He stood by her dejectedly, and she sent him flying with a repulsive, "Leave me!" The youth had too much on his conscience to let him linger. His manner of going smote her brain.

Was it credible? Was it possible to think of Alvan wounded? — the giant laid on his back and in the hands of the leech?. Assuredly it was a mockery of all calculations. She could not conjure up the picture of him, and her emotions were merely struck and stunned. If this be true!

But it can be resolutely disbelieved.

We can put it before Providence to cleanse itself of this thing, or suffer the consequence that we now and for ever quit our worship, lose our faith in it and our secret respect. She heard Marko's tale confirmed, whispers of leaden import, physicians' rumours, and she doubted. She clung insanely to her incredulity. Laughter had been slain, but not her belief in the invincibility of Alvan; she could not imagine him overthrown in a conflict — and by a hand that she had taken and twisted in her woman's hand subduingly! He, the unerring shot, laid low by one who had never burnt powder till the day before the duel! It was easier to remain incredulous notwithstanding the gradational distinctness of the whispers. She dashed her "Impossible!" at Providence, conceived the tale in wilful and almost buoyant self-deception to be a conspiracy in the family to hide from her Alvan's magnanimous dismissal of poor Marko from the field of strife. That was the most evident fact. She ran through delusion and delusion, exhausting each and hugging it after the false life was out.

So violent was the opposition to reason in the idea of Alvan's descending to the duel and falling by the hand of Marko, that it cried to be rebutted by laughter: and she could not, she could laugh no more, nor imagine laughing, though she could say of the people of the house, "They act it well!" and hate them for the serious whispering air, and the dropping of medical terms and weights of drugs, which robbed her of what her instinct told her was the surest weapon for combating deception. Them, however, and their acting she could have withstood enough to silently discredit them through sheer virulence of a hatred that proved them to be duly credited. But her savage wilfulness could not resist the look of Marko. She had to yield up her breast to the truth, and stimulate further unbelief lest her loaded heart should force her to run to the wounded lion's bedside, and hear his reproaches. She had to cheat her heart, and the weak thing consented to it, loathing her for the imposture. Seeing Marko too, assured of it by his broken look, the terrible mournfulness less than the horrible irony of the truth gnawed within her. It spoke to her in metal, not in flesh. It haunted her feelings and her faint imaginations alienly. It discoloured, it scorned the earth, and earth's teachings, and the understanding of life. Rational clearness at all avenues was blurred by it. The thought that Alvan lay wounded and in danger, was one thought: that Marko had stretched him there, was quite another, and was a livid eclipsing thought through which her grief had to work its way to get to heat and a state of burning. She knew not in truth *what to feel:* the craven's dilemma when yet feeling much. Anger at Providence rose uppermost. She had so shifted and wound about, and so pulled her heart to pieces, that she could no longer sanely and with wholeness encounter a shock: she had no sensation firm enough to be stamped by a signet.

Even on the fatal third day, when Marko, white as his shrouded antagonist, led her to the garden of the house, and there said the word of death, an execrating amazement, framing the thought "Why is it not Alvan who speaks?" rose beside her gaping conception of her loss. She framed it as an earnest interrogation for the half minute before misery had possession of her, coming down like a cloud. Providence then was too shadowy a thing to upbraid. She could not blame herself, for the intensity of her suffering testified to the bitter realness of her love of the dead man. Her craven's instinct to make a sacrifice of others flew with claws of hatred at her parents. These she offered up, and the spirit presiding in her appears to have accepted them as proper substitutes for her conscience.

## CHAPTER XIX.

ALVAN was dead. The shot of his adversary, accidentally well-directed, had struck him mortally. He died on the morning of the third day after the duel. There had been no hope that he could survive, and his agonies made a speedy dissolution desirable by those most wishing him to live.

The baroness had her summons to hurry to him after his first swoon. She was his nurse and late confidante: a tearless woman, rigid in service. Death relaxed his hold in her hand. He met his fate like the valiant soul he was. Haply if he had lingered without the sweats of bodily tortures to stay reflectiveness, he, also, in the strangeness of his prostration, might have cast a thought on the irony of the fates felling a man like him by a youngster's hand and for a shallow girl! He might have fathered some jest at life, with rueful relish of the flavour: for such is our manner of commenting on ourselves when we come to shipwreck through unseaworthy pretensions. There was no interval on his passage from anguish to immobility.

Silent was that house of many chambers. That mass of humanity profusely mixed of good and evil, of generous ire and mutinous, of the passion for the future of mankind and vanity of person, magnanimity and sensualism, high judgement, reckless indiscipline, chivalry, savagery, solidity, fragmentariness, was dust.

The two men composing it, the untamed and the candidate for citizenship, in mutual dissension pulled it down. He perished of his weakness, but it was a strong man that fell. If his end was unheroic, the blot does not overshadow his life. His end was a derision because the animal in him ran him unchained and bounding to it. A stormy blood made wreck of a splendid intelligence. Yet they that pronounce over him the ordinary fatalistic epitaph of the foregone and done, which is the wisdom of men measuring the dead by the last word of a lamentable history, should pause to think whether fool or madman is the title for one who was a zealous worker, respected by great heads of his time, acknowledged the head of the voluminous coil of the working people, and who, as we have seen, insensibly though these wrought within him, was getting to purer fires through his coarser when the final intemperateness drove him to ruin. As little was he the vanished god whom his working people hailed deploringly on the long procession of his remains from city to city under charge of the baroness. That last word of his history ridicules the eulogy of partisan and devotee, and to commit the excess of worshipping is to conjure up by contrast a vulgar giant: for truth will have her just proportions, and vindicates herself upon a figure over-idealized by bidding it grimace, leaving appraisers to get the balance of the two extremes. He was neither fool nor madman, nor man to be adored: his last temptation caught him in the season before he had subdued his blood, and amid the multitudinously simple of this world, stamped him a tragic comedian: that is, a grand pretender, a self-deceiver, one of the lividly ludicrous, whom we cannot laugh at, but must contemplate, to distinguish where their character strikes the note of discord with life; for otherwise, in the reflection of their history, life will seem a thing demoniacally inclined by fits to antic and dive into gulfs. The characters of the hosts of men are of the simple order of the comic; not many are of a stature and a complexity calling for the junction of the two Muses to name them.

While for his devotees he lay still warm in the earth, that other, the woman, poor Clotilde, astonished her compatriots by passing comedy and tragic comedy with the gift of her hand to the hand which had slain Alvan. In sooth, the explanation is not so hard when we recollect our knowledge of her. It was a gentle youth; her parents urged her to it: a particular letter, the letter of the challenge to her father, besliming her, was shown;—a hideous provocation pushed to the foullest. Who can blame Prince Marko? who had ever given sign of more noble bravery than he? He had stood to defend her name and fame. He was very love, the never extinguished torch of love. And he hung on her for the little of life appearing to remain to him. Before heaven he was guiltless. He was good. Her misery had shrunk her into nothingness, and she rose out of nothingness cold and bloodless, bearing a thought that she might make a good youth happy, or nurse him sinking — be of that use. Besides he was a refuge from the roof of her parents. She shut her eyes on the past, sure of his goodness; goodness, on her return to some sense of being, she prized above other virtues, and perhaps she had a fancy that to be allied to it was to be doing good. After a few months she buried him. From that day, or it may be, on her marriage day, her heart was Alvan's. Years later she wrote her version of the story, not sparing herself so much as she supposed. Providence and her parents were not forgiven. But as we are in her debt for some instruction, she may now be suffered to go.

# The Modern Jewish Experience

An Arno Press Collection

Asch, Sholem. **Kiddush Ha-Shem**: An Epic of 1648. 1926

Benjamin, I[srael ben] J[oseph]. **Three Years in America:** 1859-1862. 1956. Two vols. in one.

Berman, Hannah. **Melutovna.** 1913

Besant, Walter. **The Rebel Queen.** 1893

Blaustein, David. **Memoirs of David Blaustein.** 1913

Brandes, George. **Reminiscences of My Childhood and Youth.** 1906

Brinig, Myron. **Singermann.** 1929

Cahan, A[braham]. **The White Terror and the Red.** 1905

Chotzinoff, Samuel. **A Lost Paradise.** 1955

Cohen, Morris Raphael. **A Dreamer's Journey.** 1949

Cowen, Philip. **Memories of an American Jew.** 1932

Cooper, Samuel W. **Think and Thank.** 1890

Davitt, Michael. **Within the Pale.** 1903

Dembitz, Lewis N. **Jewish Services in Synagogue and Home.** 1898

Epstein, Jacob. **Epstein**: An Autobiography. 1955

Ferber, Edna. **Fanny Herself.** 1917

Fineman, Irving. **Hear, Ye Sons.** 1933

Fishberg, Maurice. **The Jews:** A Study of Race and Environment. 1911

Fleg, Edmond. **Why I Am a Jew.** 1945

Franzos, Karl Emil. **The Jews of Barnow.** 1883

Gamoran, Emanuel. **Changing Conceptions in Jewish Education.** 1924

Glass, Montagu. **Potash and Perlmutter.** 1909

Goldmark, Josephine. **Pilgrims of '48.** 1930

Grossman, Leonid Petrovich. **Confession of a Jew.** 1924

Gratz, Rebecca. **Letters of Rebecca Gratz.** 1929

Kelly, Myra. **Little Aliens.** 1910

Klein, A. M. **Poems.** 1944

Kober, Arthur. **Having Wonderful Time.** 1937

Kohut, Rebekah. **My Portion** (An Autobiography). 1925

Leroy-Beaulieu, Anatole. **Israel Among the Nations.** 1904

Levin, Shmarya. **Childhood in Exile.** 1929

Levin, Shmarya. **Youth in Revolt.** 1930

Levin, Shmarya. **The Arena.** 1932

Levy, Esther. **Jewish Cookery Book on Principles of Economy Adapted for Jewish Housekeepers.** 1871

Levy, Harriet Lane. **920 O'Farrell Street.** 1947

Lewisohn, Ludwig. **Mid-Channel.** 1929

Lewisohn, Ludwig. **The Island Within.** 1928

Markens, Isaac. **The Hebrews in America.** 1888

Martens, Frederick H. **Leo Ornstein.** 1918

Meade, Robert Douthat. **Judah P. Benjamin.** 1943

Mendoza, Daniel. **The Memoirs of the Life of Daniel Mendoza.** 1951

Meredith, George. **The Tragic Comedians.** 1922

Nichols, Anne. **Abie's Irish Rose.** 1927

Nordau, Max. **The Conventional Lies of Our Civilization.** 1895

Nyburg, Sidney L. **The Chosen People.** 1917

Pinski, David. **Three Plays.** 1918

Roth, Cecil. **A History of the Marranos.** 1932

Roth, Cecil. **A Life of Menasseh Ben Israel.** 1934

Rubinow, I[saac] M. **Economic Conditions of the Jews in Russia.** 1907

Sabsovich, Katherine. **Adventures in Idealism.** 1922

Sachs, A[braham] S. **Worlds That Passed.** 1928

Seide, Michael. **The Common Thread.** 1944

Steiner, Edward A. **From Alien to Citizen.** 1914

Untermeyer, Louis. **Roast Leviathan.** 1923

Weinstein, Gregory. **The Ardent Eighties.** 1928

Yezierska, Anzia. **Hungry Hearts.** 1920

**Yiddish Tales.** 1912

Zangwill, Israel. **The Melting-Pot.** 1932

Zunser, Eliakum. **Selected Songs of Eliakum Zunser.** 1928